GHOST RUNNER

GHOST RUNNER

A REED HADDOK WESTERN

TOM WHATLEY

SUNSTONE
PRESS

SANTA FE

*The events, people, and incidents in this story
are the sole product of the author's imagination.
The story is fictional and any resemblance to individuals
living or dead is purely coincidental.*

Cover Illustration by Anna Salsman

Sunstone books may be purchased for educational, business, or sales
promotional use. For information please write: Special Markets Department,
Sunstone Press, P.O. Box 2321, Santa Fe, New Mexico 87504-2321.

Library of Congress Cataloging-in-Publication Data:

Whatley, Tom V., 1940-
   Ghost runner : a Reed Haddok western / by Tom V. Whatley.
      p. cm.
   ISBN 0-86534-406-X
1. Indians of North America—Fiction. I. Title.

PS3573.H33 G58 2003
813'.54—dc22

                                       2003018495

Published in

SUNSTONE PRESS
POST OFFICE BOX 2321
SANTA FE, NM 87504-2321 / USA
(505) 988-4418 / *ORDERS ONLY* (800) 243-5644
FAX (505) 988-1025
WWW.SUNSTONEPRESS.COM

For
J.B., Olie, Buford, Big Neal, Rhett, and Hot Rod

1

The fire was burning low. The men of the village were involved in their nightly talk around the small blaze, wrapped in blankets to break the chill. They were unaware of the eyes that watched from the perimeter of the campfire.

The conversation ran from the corn patches planted a few weeks earlier to the irrigation that day when they opened a log gate allowing stream water to run down small ditches to the young corn. They talked of the trades with the Navajo's to the north and the Apaches to the south. The men all shared their thoughts. They spoke of hunting and fishing. They also laid out plans to build a new stone house for a couple about to be married.

The eyes that watched were eager to move. The wisdom of the person behind them made no movement. He was careful. A lot was at stake. Suddenly the wind stirred and the trees began to speak their language. A stick fell into the fire sending up sparks. The men, startled at the sudden thud, jumped back and watched the sparks fly.

It was time for the eyes to move.

When their attention returned to the conversation, the

watching eyes looked out from a blanket covering a small frame. The men laughed. One spoke, "Big Bear, your son has done it again." They shook with laughter. Unnoticed, Ghost Runner had mysteriously appeared. This was a nightly ritual for the boy of ten summers.

2

Somewhere in Northern Arizona.

The constant ripple of the small stream made it difficult for the hunter to stay awake. He had walked most of the night to get to this place. This tree had become one of his favorite hunting places. He had been there since way before the rising of the sun. He sat on a large limb parallel with the ground, hidden by smaller limbs that splattered his hiding place with brush. The deer always used the small tributary to the main stream to drink because it was well concealed. The larger stream was about two hundred paces toward the mountains.

The brush country toward the sun's resting place was where the deer always came from. It was the perfect place. The wind usually blew from the northwest. He was high enough for a good view and shot. He seldom failed to go home without meat from this place.

But the morning hours passed and there was no sign of deer. As the day wore on, he became drowsy. Realizing his best time for a kill would now be in the late part of the day, he decided to sleep. He clutched his bow to his chest with folded arms. Relaxing on the large limb, he started to drift off.

As the wind shifted a bit, he smelled the other hunter. It was why no deer had come. The deer smelled the other hunter too.

He breathed in the air and was certain. Raising himself to his knees, with his bow quietly rigged and ready, he looked in the direction the wind was blowing. He saw nothing. He spotted three likely hiding places and watched them carefully. Still nothing. He smiled a bit and thought, one of us could have slept this morning if we had known the other was here.

He broke the silence. "Go away. It is my day to hunt this place." From one of the hiding places he saw a blur of brown and the unmistakable long tail.

He almost laughed out loud when he saw the cat leave. He sat back down on the limb and reclined to sleep.

With the cat fresh on his mind, his thoughts drifted back to when he was a boy. It was another day and another cat, but it was a day that he loved to remember.

He thought back on the time when he found the cave after many attempts to follow the cat. That was long before he made his plan to count coup on the long tailed cat. He worked hard to prepare for the day. Mustering the courage was the hardest part of the task. Now, he was inside the cave.

There was the slightest rustle of movement. He then heard the low growl as the big cat entered the cave. It really was not much of a cave. He had to crawl through a small opening to get inside. Once there, it opened to a space about as big as four horses.

He had been inside three times before while the cat was

away. Each time, after leaving, he waited to see if the cat became alarmed. It never showed any indication of scenting him.

This day was different. His plan was to stay inside until the cat returned and to stay the night in the cave. He was really counting on his medicine bag to make it work.

The bag was made from the skin of a cat he killed two years earlier. No other man had touched the bag. He only touched it after washing in the running water. He kept it away from wood smoke. It always hung from a limb hidden in the brush where the wind and earth smells washed it daily.

The bag's contents were a mixture of things. He had carefully scooped up the droppings of the cat, wrapped it in leaves, and put it in the bag. He did this on numerous occasions. He did the same for leaves where the cat sprayed. He also added shed hair and stream water. The smell was pungent when the bag was opened.

Inside the cave on this day, he opened the bag enough to allow the smell to spread. He had wrapped the skin from the previously killed cat around his neck, stomach, arms and legs. He killed a rabbit shortly before entering the cave and rubbed blood and entrails on his hair, hands, and feet. Would his careful plan be enough?

He curled up facing away from the cave entrance. It was a submissive position he noticed cats taking when they interacted. The smell of the medicine bag filled the air. Then a growl, low and near, caused the hunter to tense. His knife, held tightly inside the curl of his body, was ready. He waited. The chances were good that he would not make it out alive.

The growl ceased and the silence was loud. The hunter emitted a short low growl from deep in his throat. He had practiced it for months. More silence. He heard the cat move. It was more sensing it than hearing it. He felt the warm breath of the cat on his head. The wet nose barely grazed his skin as the cat smelled his head and then moved down his back to his feet. After a few tentative licks, the cat turned and lay down. It was soon purring and sound asleep.

The hunter used his discipline to remain motionless through the night. He spent the time thinking about this thrill of a lifetime. It was more exciting than his first deer kill. While not as dangerous, he had done almost the same thing with deer by spending a day in their bedding area with six deer sleeping all around him. He now knew his cat medicine bag worked like his deer medicine bag.

Hours later, the hunter judged that it was getting close to light when the cat stretched, stood and turned to smell his guest again. Then it left the cave. The hunter waited until light spilled into the opening of the cave before he left. Outside, he chose his own path and went to the place where he kept his cat medicine bag. He left the bag and skins there and went to the stream and washed.

Afterwards he found a sunny side of a ridge and stretched out to sleep. He was proud. He would tell no one about his night in the cave with the long tailed cat. Who would believe it of a boy of only fourteen summers anyway?

The hunter drifted off to sleep enjoying the memory of his victory over the long tailed cat. Suddenly, a sound startled him awake. He lay still and listened. He heard it again. Then he knew. This sound always brought trouble. It was man sound.

He came up to his knees on the big limb, totally alert. He heard them coming long before he saw them. He already had an arrow in place. He caught their first movement when they rode over a high bank that dropped down to the stream bed. He counted them. There were ten and it was obvious that some were hurt by the way they were hanging to their saddles.

They pulled up a short distance from his tree and dismounted. The men who were not hurt helped the wounded men down. Four of them appeared to be hurt bad. The hunter wondered what had happened. He remained motionless and listened. He knew enough of their language to understand their conversations.

"Let's make camp here for the night. These boys can't ride much more in the shape they're in," one of the men declared as if it were an order.

"Who put you in charge?" another shot back. "I say we ride on and leave them. If Haddok and his bunch follows us, we'll be in a mess."

"If you had been hit, would you want us to leave you?" the first fellow spoke. "Mendoza is dead and I ain't wanting to be no boss. I just know that I ain't leaving these men. If you want to leave, then ride on. If you are staying with me, then help me get them down and see what we can do to help them. We need to get a fire going and heat up some water. One of you find a place where you can watch our back trail and somebody needs to get back up the creek a spell and let us know if we get any company from that direction."

The fellow who wanted to leave was fairly shamed into staying. The men got busy. The fire was going soon and the groans of the injured men was about all the hunter could hear. The lookouts moved out and the horses were tied to a rope stretched between two trees.

The hunter had taken it all in, a little mad at himself for being effectively treed in the middle of a white man's camp. He hoped none of his people ever learned of it. It would be a source of kidding for the rest of his life. I'll wait until it is dark and then I'll swing down and slip away, he thought.

Even though the men below were busy helping their wounded, they were obviously upset. A couple of hours had passed since they rode in. Coffee was made and the lookouts changed. Some beans were cooking and the smell almost got to the hunter. As they waited on the beans, the men began to talk.

"They were sure waiting on us at Haddok's ranch. Somebody from town must have warned them we were coming," the man who had wanted to ride on earlier said.

"Your right. I don't know how many guns they had. It sure ain't no fun riding into that kind of trap. We should have known something was a little funny about this whole setup. Twenty thousand dollars is a lot of money. If somebody is willing to pay that much to have Haddok killed, then he must be some kind of grizzly bear. The fact the offer has been out there for a spell and he's still alive ought to have made us be a little more careful. Mendoza always just run roughshod over whatever got in his way and felt like there wasn't anybody out there he couldn't handle. Well, he found one," another man added.

As they talked, it began to grow dark. The sun went down behind the high ground to the west. The hunter had been ready to leave for a while. His departure had been complicated by the fact one of the men was leaning back against a tree looking straight in his direction. He would have to wait until the man went to sleep.

The hunter suddenly grew tense. He heard a sound that

was not normal. It did not come from the camp. He pinpointed it coming from the direction of the lookout watching their back trail. It was a muffled sound and it went unnoticed by the men around the fire. He waited and listened. He heard nothing else. Suddenly the quiet of the night was disrupted by an explosion of rifle fire that came from the far side of the camp. The man leaning against the tree fell. The rifle fire continued in rapid shots cutting the men down as they tried to get out of their bedrolls. As quickly as it came, the sound of the rifle ceased. The hunter had his bow ready, expecting anything.

He saw movement. A man walked slowly into the faint light of the fire. He stood still and looked over the camp. His rifle was at the ready. Another shot rang out from the hunters right and the man who had started the shooting went down, thrown to his side by the slug that tore into his body. It was amazing that the man actually fired twice toward the flash of the shot that hit him. Then it was quiet.

The hunter heard the lookout who fired the shot from his right as he walked slowly toward the camp. The man stopped and listened. He was standing in the open and the moonlight silhouetted him perfectly. Without thinking or reason other than sensing it right to do, the hunter pulled his bowstring back to his cheek and looked down the arrow. The release was smooth and the sound almost impossible to hear. The only other sound was the arrow sinking into the chest of the man below. He fell in his tracks. The hunter swung down. He checked the camp quickly and found everyone dead. He heard the sound of a horse moving and then the thud of a body falling to the ground.

He moved quickly in the direction of the sound and found the man crumpled by his horse. The hunter knew he was bringing trouble to himself and his people, but he never hesitated. A man who would take on ten warriors alone was a brave man. He deserved to live. The hunter felt of him and found him alive. He quickly did what he could to stop the man's bleeding and lifted him to his horse. He led the horse and headed up the mountain. He would do what he could to help the brave man live. There were too few brave men in the world.

3

The hunter worked his way slowly up the mountain, holding the injured man on the horse, taking great care to leave no sign. The man groaned in pain and the hunter knew he had to get him off the horse as soon as possible. He made it to the stream running on the other side of the mountain and walked the horse into the water from a shelf of rock. The stream was flowing swiftly and the water was cold.

The hunter then headed about a half mile upstream and tied the horse to some brush hanging out over the water. The stream was waist deep on the hunter in the middle and ran shallow near the bank. He lifted the man down and laid him on a flat rock reaching out to the waters edge. He pulled the man's shirt back to reveal a ugly wound that entered his body just below the rib cage. He turned him carefully and saw there was no exit wound. In the moonlight he could see that he was still bleeding. He poured cold water from the stream over the wound from cupped hands. He then reached down into the water and found a place where sediment had collected and brought up a handful of mud, placing it on the wound and pressing tightly with his hand.

After a few minutes, he repeated the process. The man was unconscious, but his breathing was steady. He had lost a lot of blood.

Turning from the wounded man, the hunter moved back downstream staying in the water. He went just below where he had entered before and walked across the stream. He lifted his foot out of the water and planted it down in the mud. He then quickly returned to the wounded man. He knew it was a risk, but he felt the need to leave some kind of message.

When he got back, the man was breathing better. The bleeding had stopped, but he was still unconscious. He waited a while, then he put cold water on the man's face and neck. As he waited, he contemplated the danger he was putting himself and his people in.

The hunter was the leader of his village. The Apaches had gone on a raiding frenzy over ten years ago. Most of the adobe dwelling Indians that lived along the Mogollon rim had been killed or taken captive. The Hopi people, his relatives, had lived there for years hunting the woodlands and farming their patches of corn, squash, and melons.

The hunter was Moqui. His grandfather had kept the name of his ancestors when they migrated to this area.

When the Apaches began raiding, the hunter took his immediate community to the hidden valley where they now lived. His father had shown him the valley while they were on a long hunt when he was a boy. He told him to tell no one and to go there if he ever needed a safe place. He had taken eighteen people with him that day, carrying only blankets, weapons, seed, and food.

He had created a strong law among his people concerning the valley. Only one person would ever leave it at a time, and that

18

for the purpose of hunting or gathering food. The person outside the valley must choose to die before bringing or leading anyone into the valley. He had often taken great care to see that they adhered to the law. Now, he was in the process of breaking it.

If he saved the man's life, he would have to take him inside the valley. He must decide. Why should he care about this white man? What will happen to his people once they are discovered? Will he ever be able to lead after breaking a law he set? The easiest thing would be to leave this man and go home.

Yet, there was something inside him that would not let him do it. He couldn't explain it. It was as if he had been placed up in the tree to save the man's life. If his hunt had gone as usual, he would have been back in the valley with a freshly killed deer by now. The Spirit had sent the long tailed cat to change that.

The man's courage told the hunter that he was a man of strength. He heard the others talking about someone paying to have him killed. He could not bring himself to let him die. He made his decision. He would take the man into the valley.

4

The hunter was given the name Tall Tree by his father when he was born. The birth name was given for two reasons. He was such a big baby. His father, he was told, held him up for all the village to see and proclaimed, "I have been given a tall tree by the Great Spirit. Tall Tree will be his name."

The tall tree also had a special place in the legends of his people. According to the legend of the beginning of life on the world above, passed down from the ancient ones, a tree was planted in the world below and it grew so tall that it punched a hole in the crust of the surface of the world above. The Old Ones climbed the tree and squeezed through the hole. Thus began life on the world above.

For the hunter to carry the name Tall Tree was a thing of pride. He placed great respect in the legends of his people and was often told by his father, "You will be for those who follow you what the tall tree had been for the Old Ones."

Tall Tree's father carried the name Big Bear. He too was larger than all the men of the village. He was a leader and enjoyed sharing the legends of the Moqui people. Most of his people had gone to the name Hopi. Not Big Bear. He often told Tall Tree when he was young, "You are Moqui. Be proud." The Moqui were known for their basket making and their skill in making stone houses. They were friendly, yet fearless as warriors. They had a special sense of community and family. Their villages were usually small and consisted of one large family grouping. At the most a village would consist of no more than two or three families. They were excellent farmers and hunters. Their fighting was almost entirely in defense of their community.

Tall Tree had another name. It was given to him when he was about ten summers and he wore it with pride as well. The name was He Who Runs With Spirits. Its shortened version was Ghost Runner. He had earned the name by his constant quest to be in harmony with the world around him. He couldn't remember when the people of the village started calling him Ghost Runner. He knew he liked it from the start.

His father had spent endless hours teaching him about his world. He developed skills as a young boy that few of his people could equal as adults. His father knew he was special and allowed him much freedom.

Tall Tree developed a sense of smell as a lad, cataloging in his mind everything that existed in his world. He was constantly smelling of things. When an animal was killed, he smelled of its body until he could recognize the scent. Trees, plants, and flowers were always capturing his attention. He could be walking in the woods along the streams and smell the disturbed humus where some person or animal had walked. He knew the smell of rain and the smell of death. When in the woods, his nose was one of his best weapons.

He also used his sense of smell to mask his own. He used

whatever he knew to be a primary scent of his immediate surroundings to do so. He crushed the needles of the pine tree and rubbed them on his clothing when in the pine forest. He used the droppings of animals and crushed plants to do the same. He learned to be aware of the wind and how to use it. He could move more freely without fear of being seen or heard when the wind blew strong and the trees were in motion. When the wind was still, he became still too.

He also developed his sense of sight and worked as hard on being unseen as he did on seeing. He had the discipline to stand motionless for hours. It did not come easy, but he knew movement gave away his position. When checking out an area, he would methodically divide it in sections and watch each section for movement. He prided himself in seeing his adversary, whether animal or man, without being seen. He never wore any clothing that did not blend with his surroundings. He often rubbed dirt or mud on the shiny places of his face and body.

He studied the habits and patterns of all the wildlife. Birds were a constant interest to him and he learned that they afforded him a wealth of information. A woodland or prairie silent of bird sounds was a message of warning. A startled flock of birds flying up all at once was a signal that something or someone had startled them. A bird flying into a bush and about to land abruptly changing its mind and flying away signaled a warning. On the other hand, birds busy singing, feeding, and hopping about with freedom signaled that all was well.

The sudden flight of any kind of wildlife always told him that something fearful to them was present. He became harmonious with the wildlife around him and could be in their presence and not frighten them. He knew that a bear will move away from you unless it's young are threatened. A mountain lion will only attack what it feels superior to. Wolves are affected by the blood smell and their hunger, and will usually stay at a distance from a man. His knowledge of the inhabitants of his land was a tremendous advantage. Their use of the night and shadows of the day was invaluable. Their ability to move undetected was amazing to him and a special classroom for learning.

Big Bear told him in one of his learning days, "A small depression in the ground can hide a man even when there is no other cover. Movement always gives you away. When you do move, you must do it slowly. The shadows around you can hide you. Brush will do, but you have to be careful moving it or the movement will give you away. The three things that will tell an animal of your presence are smell, movement, and sound. Most men are untrained and rely upon sight. You must learn to use all three to hide yourself or find your prey."

Once when he was nine summers, Tall Tree caught a bobcat in a snare. He fashioned a cage made of strong limbs tied together by leather to hold the cat. He threw a blanket of skins over the animal and held it down while he freed it from the snare. Carefully he pushed it into the cage and closed the door. He placed the cage containing the bobcat out in an opening in the woods and then tried to sneak up on it. For weeks he used every ounce of his skill. Often he would take an entire day in his attempt to surprise the cat. It never failed. When he would finally get to where he could see the bobcat, it would be looking right at him. Finally, he walked up to the cage after an all day contest, opened the door, and let the cat go. He laughed and said, "You are the best, cat with no tail. Go and enjoy life."

As a young boy, Tall Tree never walked up to a camp or

acknowledged his presence to people who were around a campfire. He would take his time and just appear. It always prompted laughs and at times shock and fear. It became a game they all enjoyed and that Tall Tree usually won. It was the combination of all these traits and skills that caused someone to say one day, "Tall Tree must run with the Spirit." He Who Runs With Spirits was born and Ghost Runner was what everyone who knew him called him.

❖ ❖ ❖

As he sat by the injured man and continued to place cold water on his face, he looked deep into the heart of one who fought death so valiantly. Most people would already be dead. Yet this man's heart continued to beat strongly. He had not moved in some time, but life was still in him.

If Bud Haddok could have somehow seen the picture portrayed by his still body and the strong hands of a big man carefully dripping water upon his face, he would have been grateful that fate had placed a tall tree and a ghost runner in his life.

5

It was the middle of the night when Tall Tree gently lifted the wounded man to his horse. He removed the man's pistol belt. It held a well oiled pistol and a beautiful knife that Tall Tree grasped in his hands for a while and marveled at its craftsmanship. He draped these over the saddle horn and then placed the man backwards on the horse and bent him gently chest down on a blanket that he took from a bedroll on the back of the horse. He placed the blanket so it would add pressure to the wound. He tied the still unconscious man's hands around the horse's belly. When everything was in place, he started out at a slow walk.

He stayed in the stream bed for about two hours and then came out on a rocky shelf and headed west on an old trail taking him over two mountains and down into a valley where the stream that ran through their secret place flowed. He entered the stream and hung close to the eastern bank because it was deep.

He always approached their hidden valley by way of the stream. It left no tracks for anyone to find and follow. The banks of the stream were covered with head high brush and it afforded an approach no one could see unless they were high in the trees that grew along the stream.

He soon neared the entrance to the valley. He had been hearing the waterfall for some time. The waterfall always bothered him because it destroyed his ability to hear any danger sounds. Because of this, he moved slowly and deliberately. He looked around every turn of the stream for long periods before moving on.

High on the western side of the waterfall was an outcropping of rocks that reached over the sheer drop to the outside world. A large pine tree grew up beyond the outcropping. A person, while well hidden, could step out onto a limb of the tree and move to its trunk where a series of limbs joined the body of the tree. They always kept someone in that tree during the hours of light as a watchman. The watchman had a perfect view of the waterfall and the hidden entrance to the valley.

Tall Tree looked up and gave the man his signal that everything was all right. He knew he brought fear in the watchman and a warning was being sent to his people at that very moment. They had never had a horse in the valley and now their leader was bringing one in holding the body of a stranger.

Tall Tree knew his greatest task was keeping the wounded man alive. Perhaps a greater task would be explaining to his people why he had broken the law.

Tall Tree slowly led the horse to the waterfall and up on the rock shelf leading through the falling water to the passageway into the valley. The horse was a snug fit for the passageway, but they moved through it with little difficulty. When they emerged on the other side, men of his village stood with pulled bows and looks of fear on their faces.

Tall Tree told them to go tell his wife to bring water and her medicine to his cave. When he had done what he could do for the man, then he would sit in council with them and explain his actions. The men trusted Tall Tree and did what he said. He also told them to keep a special vigilance on the entrance day and night until he told them to stop. He then headed eastward up the side of the mountain until he reached the cave where he and his father had camped when he was a boy.

When he reached the cave, Tall Tree led the horse inside and back into the recesses of the mountain. Inside it was cool and dry. He untied the man's hands and removed the blanket from beneath him. There was no blood on the blanket and that encouraged him. The man still breathed smoothly.

Tall Tree placed the blanket on the rock floor of the cave and gently placed the man on the blanket. He then led the horse further back into the cave and removed the saddle.

When he returned to the man, his wife Shining Moon was there busy removing the man's clothing. She fashioned a bed of skin blankets and rolled the man over onto them. She used water from a pot others had helped her bring to the cave to wash the mud pack away that Tall Tree used to stop the bleeding. When she was satisfied the mud was removed, she made the wound bleed again. She watched it carefully until she felt it had bled enough. Then she poured a liquid substance into it and placed a paste of her own on top of the wound. She covered it with large special leaves and tied them in place around his body with strips of leather. After covering his naked body with another skin blanket, she busied herself building a small fire. Everything her hands did was with purpose and certainty. Not once did she speak to her husband or question why the man was there. Her love and trust for Tall Tree was beyond questions.

Shining Moon had been a captive of the Navajo when she

first met Tall Tree. She was of Apache blood and first laid eyes on the tall handsome Moqui when he and his father came to trade with her captors. Tall Tree saw her as well, but she was unaware she had caught his eye. When they were ready to leave the Navajo village, she learned that Tall Tree had traded for her. He said nothing to her that day and she simply followed along with them uncertain of her future.

The next day, when they arrived at the Moqui village, Tall Tree told her she was free to leave or stay. He explained to her that he never intended to own her. He wanted her to stay and hopefully she would come to the time when she would want to be his wife. From that moment she started on a course that would always have as a primary purpose the desire to please this man. Their marriage followed six moons later and she had since given him two daughters and a son.

When she had finished the immediate care for the wounded man, she left the cave. Looking back over her shoulder as she walked away, she saw the strong Tall Tree placing cool water on the face of the man. Few people knew the tender side of the man most knew as Ghost Runner. The name she used for him when no one else could hear, especially when they were in their blankets, was Tender Heart.

Shining Moon returned a short time later with two clay pots, placing them by the man. One contained water and the other contained a mixture of herbs and plants that produced a deep sleep. She knew this man's body needed rest. He was a strong man or he would not be alive. She hoped the paste and ointment she placed in and on the wound would keep infection away. She gently lifted his head and poured water into his mouth in small amounts and allowed it to seep down his throat. She did the same with her potion.

Placing them back beside the man, she left again without so much as a glance at her husband. He was in deep thought and she was sure of the reason why. Back at the village the talk had already started concerning the breaking of the law.

6

Tall Tree sat by the white man and wondered what had kept him alive. He had lost enough blood to kill most people. In his mind he figured the Great Spirit had willed it along with placing him to help. He did not know if he could explain it so the people of his village would understand.

As he sat in the cave, he remembered his father Big Bear and grandfather Bear Walk. They both shared times in their lives with him when the only explanation for events and happenings was the Great Spirit. His mind drifted to the things his father and grandfather told him about the migration of the Moqui people to where he now lived. His grandfather died when he was sixteen summers. He missed the old man's wisdom. He was sure his father had been killed in the Apache raids that had caused him to move his family to the hidden valley. If his father was alive, he would have come to the valley.

Tall Tree wished that Big Bear and Bear Walk were still alive. They understood the things concerning the Great Spirit. The men of his village did not always understand. Bear Walk told him the story of how the Moqui were led by the Great Spirit when they came from the big water at the sun's resting place. He often said the Great Spirit had given them a good place to live, hunt, and grow their crops. He also spoke of the Spirit houses, the stone houses common to the Moqui and unknown in other Indian people of their day, as one of the chief reasons his people had survived.

The houses had walls that were formed by flat stones mortared together with thin coats of sticky mud. The roofs were supported by poles that were laced with brush, small limbs, and mud. The houses were entered by the roof. An outside ladder led to the roof and an inside ladder permitted the people to climb down inside the house. The outside ladder could be pulled up when all the family was inside. The roof could also be used to defend the house. Some of the stones in the walls were left without mortar so they could be removed for ventilation and observation. The houses proved to be warm in the cold winters and cool in the heat of summer. Bear Walk told him the stone houses were the type the Great Spirit lived in and the design had been given by him to their forefathers.

The village Tall Tree was now the leader of consisted of eight such houses. When they first came to the valley their people totaled eighteen. There had been three men, their wives, and twelve children. The number now was twenty-eight. Four of the boys had become men and married. Their children had raised the number. A house for each family had been constructed and one house was for village meetings when the weather was bad. They chose a small bowl shaped hollow farther back up in the valley for the site of their village. A spring fed stream ran through it on its way to the big stream below. The houses were placed where each could be defended by the others. Cooking fires were always inside the circle of houses and a large council fire was located in the center. It was to this fire that Tall Tree would go and talk to his people before the day was through.

The village was placed well back from the entrance to the valley on purpose. Wood smoke and the noise of children would be a tragedy to his people if someone from the outside smelled the wood or cooking food. Playing children always make noise and that too could be a give away. That was not all that much to worry about, as Tall Tree soon learned. The sound of the waterfall masked any noise coming from the valley. The sound of the falling water was so deafening that it could be heard for over a mile downstream.

Meanwhile, Tall Tree spent most of the day in the cave with the white man. Shining Moon came a number of times. Each time she changed the dressing on the wound, poured more water and sleep potion down the man's throat, and bathed his face with cool water. She was a good wife and mother. She had given him two beautiful daughters, Pale Moon and Morning Light. Both were maidens and it worried Tall Tree that there was very little choice for husbands. The girls were ready, but the only suitors for them in the valley had not won their hearts. His son, Tree Wind, was only eight summers. Tall Tree was already teaching him all he knew concerning the world about him. The youngster was a fast learner and a lot like his father. The one detriment to his learning was the fact that he could not get out into the world and learn. There was some game inside the valley, but they were around the deer so much they appeared to be tame. They harvested the older ones when the weather was so bad in the winter that they could not go out and hunt. The deer were also a problem for their crops and the patches had to be watched all the

time when harvest was upon them. Tall Tree could hardly wait
for Tree Wind to get old enough to go outside the valley. Only
then would he learn about the wildlife.

Tall Tree looked at the wounded man and wondered if he
was right in bringing him to the valley. In a little while he would
have to sit at the council fire with the men of his village and explain
to them why he had broken the law. He knew it felt right to help
this man.

Then he looked out of the mouth of the cave and saw it was
dark. It was time to go. The men would be waiting.

7

When he reached the village the council fire was glowing brightly. Tall Tree walked toward the fire. All the village was present. The only person absent was his wife. She needed to hear no explanation from her husband. Her absence was a cause of pride in the heart of the big man. His two daughters were sitting with the women and girls behind the circle of men. He knew their presence was because this was an event, not because they distrusted their father. Tree Wind was also there, sitting behind the men. It was obvious to Tall Tree that he was there to support his father. His eyes and stern face gave him away.

The men seated at the council were Falling Elk and his two sons Red Elk and Big Man, along with Grey Wolf and his two sons Wolf Head and Small Deer. The men sat with their heads down and as much of their faces Tall Tree could see revealed somber expressions

Tall Tree took his seat and was silent for a long time. No one spoke or moved around the council fire. It was as if Tall Tree was in deep thought. Finally, he broke the silence.

"Today I broke the established law of bringing no outsider

to our valley. I will tell you why. I will make no excuses. After I have finished, I then will sit in your judgement. I will abide by your wishes." He looked at each of the men as he spoke. "As you know, I left the valley two nights ago to carry out my hunting responsibilities. I went to my favorite place where the waters divide at the crossing of the mountain. I was up in my tree well before light. I never fail to return with meat from this place. For some reason, the deer did not come to drink that morning. It was after the high sun when I realized why. A long tailed cat was also hunting there on this morning and the deer smelled it. I chased the cat away and decided to hunt through the late evening hours in hope of killing a deer. In the middle of the afternoon ten white men rode in quickly where I was and set up camp near my tree. Four of the men had been injured in battle. Listening to them talk, I learned that they had gone to war to kill another white man. Someone was paying them white man's money to kill him."

"I wanted to get down and leave, but I could not without being seen. I waited for dark so I could leave. I was about to leave when a single white man, the man now in my cave, walked into the camp and killed all of them but one. The one left was a watchman and he shot the man I brought to the valley. I then killed the remaining man with an arrow into his heart. I thought the lone man was dead, but when I got to him he was still alive. He lost more blood than any injured man I've ever seen, yet he was alive. It was as if he refused to die. I made the decision and brought him here for two reasons. A man so brave that he will take on ten warriors by himself deserves to live. We have too few brave men in our world. I also believe that the Great Spirit guided me. Usually I would have been back in the village with fresh meat when this occurred. The Great Spirit sent the long tailed cat to delay me and placed me where I could help a brave man. I'm sure this is hard for you to accept. Know it is the truth and it is from my heart. I am going to leave the fire and let you decide. If you wish, I will take my family and the white man and we will leave the valley. Your secret will be safe with us. I will abide by your decision."

Tall Tree stood and walked straight to his house and sat down by the cooking fire where Shining Moon was preparing his food. He had hardly settled himself when the men from the council walked over and stood above him. Grey Wolf spoke, "You are the reason we are alive today and the reason we live safely in this valley. We trust you!" With that, they turned and walked away.

Tall Tree looked Shining Moon in the eye for the first time after all the day's events and he saw her eyes smile. His smiled back. He lay back on the ground by the fire and drifted off to sleep, smelling the stew she was cooking. He may never have felt this proud of his people in all of his life.

8

Tall Tree and Shining Moon spent the first three days that the white man was in the cave watching him carefully. On the third day Shining Moon started to hold back the sleeping potion. Late on that day, while Tall Tree was feeding the fire, he heard the man groan and turned to see him open his eyes and look about. The man looked right at him and then drifted back to sleep. He told Shining Moon it was time for them to back away and let the man come awake by himself. Tall Tree told her it was his plan to never allow the man to see him. They left him unattended through the night.

When Tall Tree checked on the man the next morning, he was sleeping soundly. The clay pots had been moved during the night and it was obvious that the man had been drinking from both. This was an encouragement to Tall Tree. The man was strong and it seemed he was going to recover. Tall Tree returned to his village and told Shining Moon to take him some roasted meat. Shining Moon did so and left it by the fire. The next time Tall Tree checked on him the meat had been eaten. Shining Moon washed the white man's clothes and patched the shirt where the bullet had torn it. She then took them and placed them by the man.

Two more days passed and the man continued to eat, drink, and sleep. Tall Tree noticed where the man had also crawled a short distance and relieved himself. Tall Tree felt it would not be long until he would find him up walking around. It took a little longer than he thought, but it came five days later. Tall Tree had placed the man where he could see his bed from outside the entrance to the cave. On this morning he looked inside and the bed was empty. Tall tree placed the food at the entrance and left.

From that day Tall Tree or Shining Moon watched the entrance to the cave. A few days later the man walked outside and stood looking all around the side of the mountain. He was dressed in his clothes and was looking stronger. The next morning Tall Tree came to bring food and chuckled to himself when he found the man hiding by the entrance. Tall Tree quietly hung the sack of food on a tree where it would be in plain sight when it became light and slipped back into the brush to watch. He heard the man laugh when he saw the sack and then he heard him say, "I've only seen you for a brief glance. I don't guess I'll see you until you want me to. I want to thank you for helping me." With that, the man retrieved the sack and went back into the cave.

Two more weeks passed and the man seemed to become stronger each day. He took walks that became longer and Tall Tree was afraid he would see more of the valley than he needed to. Finally, while he was away on a walk, Tall Tree hurried and took the man's horse. He walked down the mountain leading the horse until he was almost out of sight in the brush. He waited until the man returned from his walk. He entered the cave and in a moment came back to the entrance. He looked around and spotted his horse standing in the brush. Tall Tree was concealed. The man went back into the cave for a brief moment and then returned to start walking down the hill toward his horse. Tall Tree led the horse off and started for the entrance to the valley. The man followed.

Tall Tree went through the passageway and out from under the waterfall. He walked the horse about a hundred paces from the entrance and tied it to a tree. He quickly ran to the brush and hid. In a few minutes the white man emerged from the waterfall and saw his horse. He walked over to it and stepped in the saddle. He looked all around. Then he headed his horse west, across the stream, and up the mountain before him. Tall Tree remained hidden for a long time and then he returned to the valley.

When he came out of the passage way inside the valley Shining Moon was anxiously waiting on him. She held the white man's knife in her hand. "Look He left this on our blankets. He must have left it for you."

Tall Tree took the knife from her and held it in his hands. He said, "The white man is a good man. He wanted to thank me in some way. The knife is a special one. I have never seen anything like it. I would love to wear it and use it, but I cannot. You do not thank someone for doing what is right. I must return it."

9

When Tall Tree left the valley to trail the white man, he went down the stream about a mile. He had waited three days before he began because he was afraid the white man would attract the attention of others and he did not want to endanger his people. When he got over the first mountain to the west he turned north and found his trail in the valley. It was an easy trail to follow and he made good time. He was a little confused late in the day when he came upon a place where someone had been waiting on the white man. He found where they had gone into the woods and dismounted. He followed both horses until it was dark.

He then slept through the night and started out at first light. It was late in the day when he came over a rise and saw a ranch in the distance. It took the rest of the day because he crawled a lot and used the natural depression of the land to shield himself. He stayed back in the brush until it was dark. He spotted the white man's horse in the corral and knew he was at the right place. After dark, he slipped into the barn and placed the knife on the white man's saddle, leaving it there held by a loop of leather tied around the knife handle. On his way out, he stood against the firm dirt at the wall of the barn and left one foot print in the damp earth by the place where they watered their animals. Then he headed home.

10

On the Rocking H ranch in northern Arizona Reed Haddok woke up two hours before daylight with an Indian on his mind. The last few days he had been busy trying to find the back shooter Reubin Partlow. He had gone to the Diamond Ranch after Partlow's death and spent the day with Samantha.

It was a joy to sit and talk with her. He could hardly wait for the day they could be married. She understood that he had to find the Indian who had saved his life and then he had to find the man who had put the price on his head and settle the score with him. When he rode away from the Diamond, he looked back and saw the black haired beauty waving goodbye to him and swore silently that he would finish both jobs as soon as he could.

He rode back by way of Prescott and picked up the provisions. They were things he thought he could leave for the Indian and at least let him know he was grateful. Reed put together a sack of salt, some cured meat, a sack of coffee, some blankets, a hunting knife, and a axe. They were things he felt they could use. He was not sure how he was going to get them to him. He knew he couldn't enter their secret place without an invitation and he knew he was not going to do anything to attract attention to the entrance. He planned on riding out there and just seeing how things would develop.

When he got back to the ranch Josh and Raven were sitting on the porch doing what looked to him a whole lot like courting. He grinned at Josh and said, "Man, we could lose this ranch with you spending all your time on the porch gazing into her eyes."

"You know, I was just thinking the same thing about you spending all your time riding back and forth to the Diamond. Maybe you ought to see if Mr. Forbes will let you sleep on his porch," Josh returned with a belly laugh.

Reed stepped down, hitched his horse, and climbed up on the porch to sit with the best friend he had in the world. He told Josh about his plans to leave early the next morning and see if he could make some kind of contact with the Indian. Josh asked to go with him, but he persuaded him to hang close to the ranch and make sure there were no stragglers trying to claim the price on his head. Reed told him he would be gone two days at the most and he felt like he should respect the Indian and not take anybody to their secret place. Josh understood and told him to be careful. After supper Haddok turned in early, knowing he would make an early start.

He sat on the high ground about three miles from the ranch when the sun came up. He was taking his time with the pack horse and stopping often to check the area in front and to spend a little time on his back trail. He stayed to the low ground and when he had to cross a rise he did it quickly after crawling up and glassing the country in front of him. He had grown to be real careful after realizing that twenty thousand dollars would bring a lot of crazy people looking for his hide.

He stopped late in the morning and let the horses rest while he ate some jerked beef and a cold biscuit. He judged the best he could that he was about half way to the Indian's hideout. He started back out at a slow pace and continued to watch his front and back. A plan was working its way into his mind as to how he would get the provisions to the Indian. He was moving through familiar surroundings and figured he was getting pretty close when he heard the distant roar of the waterfall. He moved down the east side of the mountain he was on and left his horses on the slope, tied up in some thick brush where he could hardly see them himself.

He shouldered the sacks that he taken off the pack rack and walked carefully the rest of the way into the valley where he figured to find the stream. When he found it, he made his way through about twenty feet of thick growth that stood well over head high. When he got to the bank of the stream, he paused and looked up and down. There was a bend about a hundred paces up the stream toward the waterfall. He could see a good ways downstream. Everything looked calm. He saw no movement. The sound of the waterfall masked any other sound so he had to rely on his eyes. He stepped into the water and shivered at its coldness, then walked quickly across the stream. The water in the middle came up to his chest. The stream was running swift and he had to work to get across.

He put the sacks into the thick brush on the east side of the stream and lowered his body into the cold water until only his eyes up was showing. He left his hat with the sacks. He moved up the stream until he could see around the bend. There was another bend about twice as far up the stream as the first one. He checked the stream and the bank on both sides that he could see. He saw nothing. He looked up in the trees and checked the area as best he could. He could make out the break in the mountains where the waterfall stood and it seemed only a short distance away. He was still crouched down in the water taking it all in when his attention was drawn to the high ground above the waterfall on the west side. The wind was still and nothing was moving, but his eyes caught some kind of movement high on the bluff overlooking the waterfall. The movement was right up against the limbs of a tall pine tree standing higher than those around it.

He watched the place for a while. He saw no other movement. Maybe it was just his imagination, he thought. However, he figured that whoever was in the valley had some way of watching the entrance. It could be that the movement he saw was their lookout getting into position. A person would have to be precisely where he was to see it, and who is going to spend a lot of time neck deep in ice cold water looking. He laughed to himself and made his way back to the sacks.

His plan was now complete. He would accept the challenge of getting the provisions to the Indian without being seen. To do it, he had to wait until it was dark. He eased up in the brush alongside the sacks and curled up around some scrub bushes to take a nap. It was getting way on toward dark when he woke up. He waited on complete darkness and all the night sounds that hang around a stream of water. There was little moonlight and his chances were good.

Haddok slipped back into the cold water and walked slowly up the stream. The area of the stream that lay just below the waterfall was very dark because of the shadows. He could hardly see his hand in front of his face. He knew time was important so he picked up his pace. He made the last hundred paces below the waterfall in quick fashion and found the slab of stone that stepped up on the ledge behind the waterfall. He shielded the sacks the best he could when he went under the water because wet salt and coffee ain't worth much. Behind the fall, he eased his way down until he could feel the draft of air coming through the passageway. He then felt the passage itself.

He walked about three steps into the passage and took the axe and wedged it high against both sides. He then hung the sacks over the axe. With that, he retraced his route all the way to where he first entered the stream. He was careful to leave no sign coming or going. As he made his way back through the thick brush that lined the stream, he stopped and placed his foot in a soft depression and left one solid footprint. He smiled to himself and thought, here's your sign. He went to his horses and left. He stopped on the western slope of a mountain a good ways from the waterfall and slept the rest of the night. It was mid afternoon when he rode back into the ranch yard at the Rocking H.

11

The next week and a half Haddok caught up on the things he needed to do around the ranch. They were moving cattle to better grazing and getting as much hay as they could laid in at the ranch and other strategic places. The task of carrying cattle through the winter caused most of the work on a ranch during the summer in this part of the country. If you didn't do it, you could lose them.

Josh and Reed led different bunches of cowhands in getting the job done. When Reed came back to the ranch at night he fully expected to find the sacks of provisions he took to the Indian hanging in the barn. It didn't happen and he felt good knowing that his friend had decided to keep them. He had another trip planned for tomorrow that would allow him to take something else he thought his friend might need.

He left the ranch well before daylight and made his way back toward the valley. He took no pack horse with provisions this time. He had another plan. As he neared the boundary of the ranch he cut north for about a mile to a range where they moved cattle earlier in the week. He put a loop on two calves ready to be weaned. One was a heifer and the other a bull. He fashioned two halters from rope and tied them with a rope leading to his saddle horn. When he started out leading them, he had to pull them for about a quarter of a mile. They soon got the idea and started walking along behind him. He kept a slow pace so they could keep up. They cried and whined until they got out of earshot of their mama's. Finally they quieted down and kept up the pace. He stopped frequently to let them rest.

It was near dark when he got to the place where he left his horses on his first trip to the valley. This job was going to be a lot harder. He figured out a way to get the calves inside the valley. He just didn't know if it would work. The sound of the waterfall would help. If the calves would cooperate, the job would be easy. If they didn't, then he might do more harm than good.

After dark, he took a sack and tied it over the head of the first calf. He threw it down and tied it's front legs together and did the same for the back legs. He figured the calf to weigh about one hundred and fifty pounds. It was not unusual for them to weigh three hundred pounds at weaning, but he had chosen these because they were small. They were already eating plenty of grass and they would make it fine without their mother's milk.

He then lifted the calf and threw it around his neck, holding it's feet in front of him. It kicked a little and then settled down. The sack over the eyes was helping. He had counted on that. He walked down the slope to the water and made his way through the brush and into the stream. He was as cautious as he could be with a calf hanging on his back. Surprisingly, the trip to the waterfall was easy. He made his way behind the fall with the calf kicking at the sudden drenching it took when they went under. He took it into the passageway and cut the ropes around it's feet.

He then removed the sack and halter. He held the calf by one ear until he was finished and then gave it a slap on the rump. It bolted ahead through the passage and into the valley.

He then made his way back and repeated the same process with the second calf. It went just as easy except for when he slipped and went under in the middle of the stream. He laughed at the thought of someone watching him wrestling with the calf while trying to get his feet back under him. When he released the second one, it went racing through the passageway as well. He didn't realize how tired he was until he made it back to his horse and headed out. His body had still not completely recovered from the gunshot wound and little things like carrying a calf five hundred yards pointed that out to him. He rode a while, stopped and tied his horse in the brush, and rolled up to sleep soundly until daylight. It was late in the afternoon when he returned to the ranch.

12

A week later Haddok started out on his third trip to the hidden valley. He left early and led a pack horse loaded with more blankets, cloth, a large number of different colored buttons, ribbons, and thread. He thought the women of the valley would enjoy them. He also had some cured meat and salt. The trip was getting easier to make and he had a timetable down that put him where he always left his horses a little before nightfall. He got there on schedule and waited for it to get dark.

He spotted some tracks of unshod horses before he got to the spot where he tied his horses and he was being extra careful. The tracks looked to number enough to count for about ten horses. If they were Apaches, it spelled danger. He figured them to be Apaches because they roamed this part of the country.

After dark he made his way with the sacks hanging around his neck. When he got down to the stream he headed straight for the waterfall. The moonlight was bright and he hung to every shadow he could find. The thought occurred to him that if his hunch was right about the Apaches they could be camped somewhere along the stream. He hoped it was not near the waterfall. When he got to where he could see it, he saw no fires or any indication of a camp. He was relieved.

He made the waterfall and went behind it, heading straight to the passageway to leave the sacks. He dropped them off and went back under the fall and into the stream. As he moved back along the shadows of the eastern bank of the stream, he was shocked into a frozen position by the sight of an Indian standing quietly at the edge of the thick brush. He stood completely still and watched the shape of the body for any movement. Suddenly he noticed an arm beckoning him to come. He moved slowly, knife in hand, toward the Indian. When he got about ten paces from the figure, he realized it was a woman. He walked on and she led him back into the brush. She stopped and waited for Reed to come close. When he walked up to her, she spoke in broken English.

"I am Shining Moon, the wife of Tall Tree, who helped you. I need your help." Her voice was hardly above a whisper and he had to lean close to hear her over the sound of the waterfall.

"I am Reed Haddok. Your husband saved my life and I will help you any way I can," he responded in a whisper.

"Tall Tree left the valley early this morning to go hunting. Shortly after he left, our watchman saw a party of Apaches cross the stream just below the waterfall. A little later he heard a shot from a rifle and I am afraid my husband has been killed or wounded."

"I will look for him and help him," he quickly answered.

"I must explain to you that we have an established law that only the men can leave our valley, and that for the purpose of hunting. I am breaking the law by being here. I hoped you would come. The law requires that one would die before he would lead someone to our valley. It is our only place of safety and the men understand that. They know there will be no help from the village if they get into trouble. Tall Tree, if wounded, will lead the Apaches away from here and he will die before he tells of our village. He broke the established law when he brought you here. Were it not for the respect that our village has for him, we would have been made to leave."

"That makes me appreciate what he did for me even more. I could never repay him for saving my life. Maybe it is my turn to save his. You return to your village and know that I will look until I find him, dead or alive. I will bring him home to you." He touched her shoulder with a firm grasp as he spoke and she gently touched his hand, then quietly vanished from sight as she slipped out of the brush.

Reed returned to his horses with his mind turning in circles. He could do nothing until daylight, but he would spend a while getting ready for tomorrow. He packed a small sack with some jerked beef, tied his boots over the saddle horn of his horse, put on some moccasins that he carried for such occasions, and turned the horses toward home. He sent them running with a slap. They would return to the ranch and Josh would know that he sent them. They knew each other's actions that well. He would not come looking. He would simply know that Reed was up to some footwork and horses would be in the way. Reed could look for him to bring a ride in a few days. With that done, he tried to sleep. The thought of his friend out there somewhere wounded and eluding ten Apaches kept him awake. He thought, hang in there buddy and do your best. I'm coming. He now had a name from his friend. Tall Tree. That sounded like him. He also had a name for his wife. Shining Moon was a beautiful name. He could barely see her face in the dark, but he knew the touch of her hand. It had been her hands that cared for him in his time at the cave. Something in his brain had cataloged that touch. He owed her almost as much as her husband. He would bring her husband home if it cost him his life.

13

Tall Tree left the valley later than usual on the morning he had his encounter with the Apaches. He was going on a long hunt on the other side of the mountains. He planned on two days travel and one day of hunting. He did this often to conserve the wildlife closer to his village. Upon leaving the waterfall, he made his way down the stream about a half mile and then started up the first mountain. The danger zone of the noise from the waterfall got him into trouble. He stopped to check the area out in front of him and missed the lone Apache who stood back on a shelf of rock checking the back trail of his war party.

Unknown to Tall Tree, the war party had been on a raiding frenzy for two days. The lone Apache caught the movement of Tall Tree and raised his rifle as he walked out of the tall brush along the stream. Tall Tree disappeared behind some trees and did not come into view again until he was about half way up the mountain. The Apache raised his rifle, but before he could fire Tall Tree again went into the brush. The Apache now knew that he must move back up the mountain or the Indian would disappear over the top before he could get off a shot. The Apache's heart was racing because he recognized the Indian by the talk around their campfires. This had to be the one called He Who Runs With Spirits.

The Apache walked quickly up the mountain, keeping his eyes on the brush. He hurried to a spot where the brush ended at the top of the draw the man was climbing. He knelt and put his rifle on that spot. When Tall Tree came out of the brush he was walking in full stride. Only a few steps and he would be over the crest of the mountain. The Apache rushed and fired. He knew he hit the man because the blow of the bullet had thrown him over a small rise and out of sight. The Apache let out a shrill yell and ran toward where the man had fallen. He knew the sound of his rifle would bring the others racing back. He was proud of his victory over He Who Runs With Spirits.

As he ran, his thoughts stopped him dead in his tracks. He walked quickly back to where he fired the shot and then up over the mountain to retrieve his horse. He wanted to be sitting on his horse over the dead legend when his brothers came up to him. When he got his horse, he rode down to where the man had fallen. Nothing.

The leaves were covered with blood and a blood trail led south along the flat terrain just under the crest of the mountain. He was off his horse checking the trail left by the wounded man when his war party rode up.

14

The bullet hit Tall Tree with the force of a horse kick. It threw him to the side. When he fell he was below the shooter's line of sight. He looked quickly at his leg. The bullet hit him high on his leg and had gone all the way through, coming out a little higher up. He did not think it had broken the bones in his leg. It was bleeding, but he had no time to stop it. He crawled a few feet and tried to get up. The best he could do was drag the leg. He could put just enough pressure on the leg to push off a little.

Tall Tree made his way along the mountain for a few hundred paces until he saw what he was looking for. He was leaving enough blood for anybody to trail. He had to get the Apaches off their horses. It would slow them down enough for him to get somewhere and treat his wound.

He went into the brush heading down toward the stream. It was so thick he had to get down and crawl. A small trickle of water was running down the draw from a spring and when he got to it, he cupped water in his hands and drank as much as he could. He could hear the yelping of the Apaches as they started on his trail. They would be like ants after honey in a few minutes.

He knew his tactics could slow them some because they would be reluctant to move too quickly in the brush. They knew he was alive and could be waiting for them.

Lower down the draw he saw a young pine that grew thick down low to the ground. He took his bow and quiver of arrows and thrust them high into the limbs. If the Apaches didn't look up, they might miss them. He could come back for them later. His next goal was to get to water. He was growing weak from the loss of blood and had to stop the bleeding. Besides that, fresh blood on leaves shines like a ray of sunshine. He had to destroy their ability to track him so easily. When he reached the water's edge, he didn't worry about how much sign he left entering the water. The cold water felt good to his leg. The shock of the bullet had worn off and now there was only pain. Excruciating pain. When in the water, he moved to the middle of the stream and let the current carry him along. His eyes were searching for one of those places he had noted in his mind many times. He saw it and moved toward the west bank.

A large pine tree had grown near the stream and it's roots caused some of the bank to cave off. The spider web of roots reached out into the water. Tall Tree stopped and reached down to get two hands full of mud. He raised himself out of the water and onto the roots where he packed the mud into both wounds on his leg. He pulled a strip of leather from his waist and tied it over the mud, pulling it tight. He then slipped back into the water and squeezed his way into the roots.

Way back under the big tree he found what he was looking for. A large root reached across the water parallel with it and it was large enough that it ran at least a foot beneath the surface of the water. Tall Tree ducked under it and brought his body up to the surface. He propped his good leg up on other roots and wrapped his arms around some behind his head. He could hold most of his body out of the water this way. There was no way the Apaches could see him and the only way they could find him was by coming under there. Tall Tree held his knife in his hand. If the Apache came, he would not leave. Tall Tree waited for their search.

15

It took only a matter of minutes before Tall Tree heard the Apaches on the stream bank. They were talking rapidly. He could not make out what they were saying. He could speak their language well from his trading days with his father and from his teacher Shining Moon.

Tall Tree's thoughts went to his wife and his children. He had to survive for them. He was fighting the physical fatigue that comes from losing so much blood. He knew he could drown if he passed out. No one would ever find his body wedged into the roots. He tried to shift his position. He could not find a better one. Instead, he held tight and hoped they would leave before he became so weak that he passed out.

The Apaches began to search the banks of the stream and the brush that ran out from the banks. Some of them crossed over and were on the same side as Tall Tree. They talked among themselves and they felt he went down stream. They surmised it would be easier for him while wounded. They knew he could be floating way ahead of them by now, but they would leave no hiding place unturned. The Apache who shot Tall Tree described him to the others and they were sure the man they were trailing was He Who Runs With Spirits. He would be a trophy for the entire village. The older ones had known him from when he came along with his father to trade with them. He had become a lasting enemy when he took an Apache woman for a wife. They had heard over and over how the Apache woman now had the heart of a Moqui.

The brush along the stream banks was searched thoroughly for sign. The Apaches found no reason to believe He Who Runs With Spirits had left the stream. Could it be that the Spirits had taken him away. They were very superstitious and some of the younger ones were not sure they wanted to come up to him alone. Tall Tree never imagined his second name would one day help him evade his enemies.

The three Apaches on Tall Tree's side of the stream eventually came to the large tree where he was hiding. He heard them talking and could understand them.

"He could be under the tree," one of them said.

"I'll see," another said as he cut a small sapling to use as a prod.

Tall Tree heard the splash as the Indian came into the water. His body became tense as he lifted himself higher behind the large root. He felt the surge of water and the sound of the stick being pushed into the roots below him. Once the stick barely grazed his rear end and he quietly raised it up a little.

"He is not under here," the man with the stick shouted to the others. "If he was, he would be dead by now. No man could stay under the water that long, even He Who Runs With Spirits."

They laughed and moved on down the stream. Tall Tree relaxed for a moment and then he heard them returning.

"I'm going under the water to see," an Apache said. "We cannot let him escape."

"Go if you like," the man who had been in the water said. "I would have gone under the water myself, but I was afraid he was dead. If he is dead, then the Spirits who run with him might be there guarding his body. I felt nothing with the stick and I saw nothing that made me think he was under there."

The man who was determined to go under the water sounded less determined when he responded, "If you checked, there is now no reason for me to look."

Tall Tree smiled to himself and thought, you are a wise Apache. Your friend just saved your life and mine.

They moved away and this time they did not return, but Tall Tree would wait for darkness to come. He would then move out into the stream and ride its current. In the meantime, he busied himself thinking thoughts of his family and the white man. He also mapped out his plan of escape. The pain in his leg worsened and it required all the discipline he could muster to remain in place. He moved within his mind, as he often did while hunting, and put his body into nonexistence. He would not grow tired and he would not pass out. He would will that away by his own strength. Tall Tree would live and sit again at the cooking fire of Shining Moon and at the council fire of his people. Thinking strong thoughts, the hours of the afternoon drifted by like the current of the stream outside his hiding place.

When darkness came, Tall Tree eased his body into the water and out from under the roots. He held himself there and looked up and down the stream. The sound of the waterfall was still strong so he was not sure of his hearing. Seeing no fires, he pushed himself out into the stream and began to float, half submerged, downstream. He worked to keep himself in the middle. He had rounded a couple of bends in the stream when he spotted the first flicker of the Apaches' campfire. They were on the eastern bank. The fire was about three hundred paces down stream from him. He stopped by putting his good foot down. He studied the situation.

It was a dark night and the stream was in the shadows of the trees that lined it. Even if they had someone watching the stream, he would be hard to see. He determined his best action would be to stay in the water and drift by quietly. He released himself and let the current take him. To his surprise, the stream became shallow and he had to force himself to stay beneath the water. That was why they chose this spot to camp. For him to get by, he would have to expose himself.

He stopped again and tried to judge by the sound of the stream just how shallow it was. He could see a few places in the dim light where water was running around rocks. All of those places were closer to the Apaches. The water seemed to run deeper over against the western bank. Tall Tree was sure the strength of the current had washed the sediment from that side and it would be where he would pass. The thought then occurred to him that the deep side would be where they would place someone to watch.

He eased over close to the western bank and allowed himself to inch closer to the place where the fire was opposite him. He stopped and took a long time looking on the western bank. It took a while, but the watchman finally moved. He was up on a limb of an overhanging tree. He could look straight down on the water. Tall Tree was in a dilemma. What could he do?

After a few minutes of study, he moved forward quietly.

When he was thirty paces from the watchman, he stopped again and listened. He could see movement in the camp and hear the Apaches talking. They seemed to be placing their trust in the watchman. He hoped there was only one. That thought caused him to stay longer and search each area of the banks with his eyes.

Certain there was only one, Tall Tree breathed in long and deep and then slipped beneath the water. He pulled himself, using the good leg and his arms, down to the bottom. With strong pulls and guiding kicks he stayed as close to the bank as possible. He went right below the watchman.

Tall Tree's lungs were about to burst when he raised his head out of the water about twenty paces beyond the watchman. He let out a controlled gush of air and breathed in quickly the fresh night air. The watchman seemed to have noticed nothing. Tall Tree again allowed the current to carry him and he floated away from the camp.

The thought occurred to him that he would enjoy telling his son Tree Wind about this experience.

16

Haddok was awake, waiting for it to get light enough for him to see. He had slept off and on through the night. It was hard to sleep while thinking about his Indian friend out there needing help. He was hoping that the shot his people heard had not hit him. If the Apaches missed, then Tall Tree was simply taking them on a journey away from the valley. If he was hit, and still alive, he could be captured or wounded so badly that he needed his help desperately. Reed waited until he could see well enough to be careful and still get the job done. He then headed out.

Haddok was traveling light. His hat and boots went along with his horse. All he had was a small sack with some jerked beef and a couple of biscuits. He moved down to the stream and crossed over. After checking the area out for any movement, he worked his way down the edge of the brush lining the stream. He went downstream about a quarter of a mile and found where he thought Tall Tree might have come out heading east. A little way out of the brush he found a small indentation in the soil that appeared to be a moccasin footprint. The line of travel seemed to be going straight up the mountain. The route was through a thick stand of trees and then into thick brush that grew in the bottom of a narrow draw that pointed its way toward the top. He found a slight trail there indicating it had been traveled more than once. Tall Tree could have gone this way. He slowly went on up until the brush faded out at the top of the draw. From there it was only about fifty paces to the crest of the mountain.

Reed stood back in the brush and looked the entire landscape over. He saw and heard nothing. He stepped out and headed for the crest, but pulled up as his heart sank. There was sign all over the ground. Unshod hoof prints were everywhere. The leaves and ground was torn up from all the movement. But that was not what caused his heart to sink. In the midst of all of this was sure sign that Tall Tree had been hit. Blood was everywhere and small bits of bloody flesh still attracted swarming flies.

It was apparent that he had crawled a few feet and then got up to walk. The blood trail was clear as was the fact that he was dragging one leg. Reed's hope was raised. If he could get somewhere and get the bleeding stopped, he could survive. Could he do that? He had about ten Apaches after him and could hardly walk. The chances were good he was in the hands of the Apaches. Reed wanted to hurry, but he knew it could get him killed. He had to take his time and do it right. This was his only chance of helping.

He followed the trail and had no trouble with all the blood. Even without the blood, the Apaches were leaving him a good trail. He went south beneath the crest of the mountain for a few hundred yards and then took a downhill turn into some of the roughest brush he had ever seen. It covered another draw much like the one he came up and it led back toward the stream. Reed thought, he's plenty smart. He's making them get off their horses and he's headed for the one thing that can stop the bleeding. Cold water!

Reed followed the trail into the brush and had to get down and crawl on his hands and knees in places. He could tell the Apaches followed Tall Tree. Their sign was clear. The blood trail was also still there. The blood sign led out of the draw, through the brush along the stream, and stopped where Tall Tree entered the water. It had been easy until now. Trailing a man in water is hard to do. All you can do is work both sides of the stream until you find where he left it. Reed felt sure his friend went downstream because he would not lead them toward the hidden valley. He sat still in the edge of the brush and studied the situation for a spell. He had to be very careful. If Tall Tree was successful in keeping away from the Apaches, they would definitely be looking for him along the stream. He had to find him. He also had to keep from being found.

After a spell of looking and listening, Reed eased out in the water and walked slowly along the edge. He kept as low in the water and as close to the brush as he could. Every twist and bend in the stream stopped him for a time of looking and listening. All along the way he was looking for a place where Tall Tree could have hidden. His wound would have caused him to find a quick hiding place and he didn't think he would have traveled far without getting caught without it.

He noticed the big tree with the roots growing out into the water and marked it as a place to check. He slipped out of the water on both banks a short way back and had found Apache sign all over. It meant that they had not found him up to this point and were scouring the sides for any sign. His bleeding would certainly leave sign if he came out of the water.

Reed moved down across from the big tree and stopped to check for movement. Feeling that it was clear, he moved across to the tree. There was sign all around that the Apaches had checked the place. Reed saw where a sapling had been cut and it was lying on the bank. They probably used it to punch around under the roots.

He ducked under and went inside the mangle of roots to find that Tall Tree could have hid under there and not be found. If he did, he probably stayed there and let them move on. On that assumption, Reed had to decide which way Tall Tree would have gone when he came out.

His instinct told him he would not have left the water and he would not have gone upstream. Both would have been dangerous for him or his village. Reed believed he stayed with the stream and probably waited for dark and tried to get past them. If that was it, his friend and ten Apaches were in front of him. It was about noon by this time so he hid himself. He nibbled on some jerked beef and let the sun move enough to leave shadows along the stream. He would need them as he made his way downstream.

17

Tall Tree allowed the current to take him away from the Apache camp. He soon lost track of distance because the stream was winding and he could not measure how far he had gone in a normal fashion.

He had been in the water about two hours when he saw what he was looking for. Along the eastern bank was a slab of flat rock about a foot out of the water. It stuck out over the stream and was covered with brush. He made his way to it and carefully pulled himself up.

As soon as he was out of the water he began to shake. Weakness came over him and he knew he had to find a place to hide quickly. He crawled under the brush and pushed out a place to hide. He could not stop shaking so he curled up like a dog to try and stop it. He felt his face and it was hot to the touch, even though his body was shivering. He knew he had a fever and it caused him to lose consciousness periodically. When he was awake, he was delirious.

The sun had been up a couple of hours when the Apaches found the mud and blood smudges on the rock. Tall Tree never heard the shrill yelp when the Apache warrior found him. He never felt the pain when they dragged him out. He was close to death.

The warrior who found him felt proud. He declared to his fellow Apaches, "It will be told for a long time around our campfires that White Fox captured He Who Runs With Spirits. I will be known forever."

Four of them carried the limp body of Tall Tree back toward their camp. They stopped occasionally to rest. The big Indian was heavy. Never had they thought they would be able to go back to their village with such a victory. He Who Runs With Spirits had long been considered a prized trophy. They were happy and yelling like children.

They talked along the way about the great reception they would get from their people. The four Apaches were all young warriors and wanted the respect of the older men. He Who Runs With Spirits had been a main conversation around their camp fires on many nights when they were young boys. There was some thought among the elders that he might indeed be a Spirit. Yet they were carrying his body and it was indeed the body of a real man.

When they neared the camp, others came to meet them. They took the unconscious body up beside their fire and lowered it to the ground. All of the Apaches stood around in silence for a few minutes.

"Who found him?" an older warrior asked.

"White Fox found him along the water. He had crawled up into the brush. He offered no fight. He is just as he was found," another young warrior said as he motioned to White Fox.

White Fox swelled with pride and added, "I found the sign

of his blood on the rock where he left the water. He was no match for my skill of tracking."

"Blue Dog, what are we to do?" the first warrior to speak asked.

Blue Dog, the oldest and the leader of the small group, responded, "We will do what we can to care for his wounds first. It would be much better for us if we take him back alive. We will enjoy the time when He Who Runs With Spirits is put to the test at our village. If we let him die, then we will just take a dead body and that will be it. If we take him alive, the entire village will enjoy him. Our bravery and glory will be talked about for a long time. Heat some water and make medicine to care for his wounds." With that, Blue Dog walked over and took a seat away from the warriors.

When the water was hot, they washed his wounds and made a paste of crushed leaves they had gathered. The paste was placed on the wounds and wrapped with strips of leather. When they finished, they pulled his body over to a small tree where they tied strips of leather to his hands and then around the tree. It was done in a way so he could not get his hands together. Afterwards, they walked over to sit with Blue Dog and stare at the big man they now held captive.

Blue Dog spoke. "I think it is important that we tell the village we have captured He Who Runs With Spirits. I will send someone to tell them and the rest will stay here with him. I know all the warriors will come to see what we have done."

"It was my rifle that wounded him," Running Horse said quickly. "I will go with the news."

"I found him and captured him," White Fox responded in shock. "I should be the one who goes to tell them."

Others began to talk and argue among themselves about who would go. They all wanted to take the news. Blue Dog was aware that he was the leader and if anyone was to get praise from the elders, it should surely be him. He listened to them for a few minutes and then said, "I will go with White Fox and Running Horse to take the news to our village. The rest will stay here and guard our Spirit man and make sure he does not fly away in the night." They all laughed.

With that, one of the warriors walked over to playfully kick Tall Tree in the back and then jumped back as if scared. Again they laughed. Blue Dog continued, "I want you to keep him alive. The elders will want to know where his village is so we can go and take all he has. We will leave now. We should be back here before it is dark tomorrow. Red Hawk, I am leaving you as leader." He looked at one of the young warriors as he spoke and the appointment as leader was an obvious source of pride with the young Apache. "Put your guards out and let no one surprise you. There may be Moqui warriors looking for him. Do not shame us."

"Do not worry, Blue Dog," Red Hawk responded. "He will be here and he will be alive."

Red Hawk moved quickly to get some cold water and began placing it on the captive's face. He forced some of it down his throat. He took a seat by the big man and continued to cool his face and neck with the water. Blue Dog and his two young warriors mounted their horses and rode out. Red Hawk put out his guards and gave orders for others to get food prepared.

His attention then returned to the man he intended to keep alive.

18

Reed stayed in the brush, shaded by its thick growth, until the middle of the afternoon. His clothes soon dried and the afternoon heat felt good. The sun moved over its highest point and was now moving toward the west. The entire stream bed was washed in shadows, except for an occasional spot where the sunlight broke through the trees. He could now move down the stream and make use of the shadows to hide himself.

He spent the time waiting with mixed feelings. He was sure his friend needed him. It was hard to wait. He was also sure he could not help if he was dead or captured. Better judgement won out and he waited for the shadows.

Then Reed slipped quietly into the water and moved slowly down the eastern bank. He kept a low silhouette and took cautious steps on the rocky bottom. This kind of travel was slow and interrupted by periods of cautious stopping. He spent almost an hour on the first three hundred paces. Then the stream made a sharp bend to the east.

When he reached the bend, he moved across to the west side. He could then see around the bend. He studied the water, banks, and trees for any sign of movement. He was about to move when something caught his eye. He froze. His tension was relieved when two deer lowered their heads to the water and began to drink. The wind was from the northwest and he was certain they would smell him. They did not. After a little while, they turned and walked back into the brush undisturbed. He felt better because he figured the deer would have alerted him if anyone was down the stream. From his position he could see the stream went about five hundred paces before it made another turn to the west. He started to move again. This time he hung close to the western bank.

He used up another hour or so getting to the next turn in the stream. He was just about to cross to the other side to see around this bend when he heard a series of yelps. He was certain they were made by the Apaches. He immediately got out of the stream on the west bank and crawled into the brush. He fully expected them to come around the bend at any moment. It didn't happen. The rapid high pitch yells continued for a few minutes and then there was silence.

He remained motionless. He didn't want to shake any of the brush so the Apaches could see the tops moving. Another hour passed. At times he could hear the Indians talking. They had either stopped here or returned to a camp. The excitement they were showing bothered Reed. Without looking, he was certain they captured or killed Tall Tree.

He used the time to try and think. By the sound of the stream he figured he was on a narrow finger of land caused by its abrupt turn. It sounded as if there could be no more than thirty paces to the stream across the finger. If this was the case, he was lying only a few paces from a bunch of Apaches who were more than likely holding his friend.

The sun was getting low and about to drop behind the high ground to the west. He figured he'd better move to where he could get the layout of their camp before it got dark. He slowly slid on his belly in and around tall bushes and clumps of brush. Dead fall was everywhere from high water. He was lucky that most of it had decayed and made little sound as he crawled over it.

He froze as he sighted movement. It was thick in there and he could not see well. He moved a little and found a spot where he had a clearer view. He was right. It was the Apache camp. They had a fire going. He was well hidden. Unless he made a sound or an abrupt movement, he felt like he was safe for the time being.

He could count ten Apaches. Their horses were tied off to the side. The fire was burning big and he could smell food cooking. They were gathered around the fire. It seemed they were in a deep discussion. One of the Indians got up and walked over to kick something on the ground. It was Tall Tree. The Indian who kicked him jumped back in mocked fright and all the others laughed. He then returned to the fire and sat down. They were making fun of his injured friend.

Reed was happy Tall Tree was still alive. He knew his wounds were serious from the amount of blood lost. It had not taken him long on Tall Tree's trail before he had won his respect. While seriously wounded he had taken ten Apaches on a long journey. He was good. Reed knew now what he had to do. He just didn't know how he was going to do it.

He continued to watch and saw three of the Indians mount up and ride away from the camp. They headed east. Soon after, two of the warriors left the camp in separate directions. One came up the eastern side of the stream opposite Reed's position and moved to some high ground where he could watch any approach to the camp. He sat down at the base of three large trees and kept his attention on the stream. Reed made a mental note of the three trees and the best approach to them. He would be going there after dark.

The other warrior went south from the camp and climbed a small ridge that would give him a good view of anyone coming from that direction. Reed lost him about midway up the ridge. He made note of the route he took and the lay of the land on that ridge. It would be hard to get to him from the stream. It would be harder to get to him by walking through their camp. His best bet would be to get higher up and come down the ridge where he figured him to be.

He looked back at where they had Tall Tree. He was tied to a small tree. He was a little up hill from the campfire and in a small depression that almost concealed his body. Reed caught some movement from him every now and then and it gave him hope. They were trying to help him. They took water to him often and one of the warriors sat beside him tending to him. They wanted him alive. That was in Reed's favor.

Well Bud, Reed thought, you got yourself a night's work cut out for you. You got seven Apaches and a wounded friend you've got to deal with. You can do it. Reed smiled a mite and remembered wondering how he would ever be able to thank the Indian who saved his life. Now he knew. He laid still and hoped for a dark night.

19

Haddok waited until it was good dark before he made his move. It was very dark down in the low ground along the stream. The trees and the mountains shielded even the slight moonlight of the young nightfall.

He laid back in the brush and listened to his stomach growl while he watched the Apaches eat. He didn't know what they were eating, but it sure beat the heck out of what he had. After a spell they relieved the guards and let them eat. He didn't know how often they might do that and it was giving him a little problem in his planning. Another problem he had to deal with was not knowing when the warriors who left might show up with a larger party. It was important that he move early and do his work as quick as possible. His plan was to take the guards first and then try and get the others while they were sleeping. He knew all his plans could turn upside down with one scream. Then he'd just have to let it all fly.

Tall Tree moved around a little while Reed was watching them eat. The remaining light just before dark allowed him to study Tall Tree's position carefully. He couldn't see all of him. He caught the movement of his arms one time and thought he saw his head raise up to look at the Apaches around the fire. He was hoping Tall Tree was conscious. Tall Tree's knowledge of the area would be a real help if he had to lose the Apaches.

Reed waited a little while after dark and let the Apaches settle down. They all wrapped up in blankets close to the fire. When he did move, he retraced his crawl to where he left the water. He eased into the current and made his way directly across the stream. When he reached the bank, he crawled up and down a little until he found a place to get out of the water without making a racket. When he got up on dry land, he took off his shirt and pants. His drawers were a dirty blue color and he figured they'd do fine. He belted his pistol belt and knife over the drawers. Cupping a handful of mud, he rubbed it over his face and all of his body he could reach.

He left there crawling straight through the brush. He took his time and tried not to do anything that would make a sound. He hated to go off and leave his clothes. I'd be in a mess if I had to hightail it and face Josh with nothing but my drawers, he thought. I'd never live that down. It's kind of funny what a man will think about at a time like this. When he got to the edge of the brush, he laid there for a minute and let his eyes adjust to the dark. He could make out the three big trees where he figured one of the guards was located. He would be first.

The trees were about a hundred paces to his left front. If he was right, the Indian would be looking away from Reed's direction. The fire at the camp was burning lower now and it had been quiet there for a spell. Reed waited a little longer to let any noise he might have made getting through the brush to die down.

If the guard had heard him, he sure didn't want him looking in his direction.

Reed then left the brush in a low crawl. He felt the ground before he put his arms and legs down. If he snapped a dead branch from one of the trees, then it would just be cut loose time. He had to make this thing work for Tall Tree. It was slow. He stopped often to listen. He had not heard any movement out of the guard. If he was where Reed thought, then he was sure getting close enough for him to hear.

Reed got to within ten paces of the first tree and stopped. He looked hard, but couldn't see a thing that looked like an Indian. It was real dark where the Indian should be and for all Reed knew the guard could be looking right at him. With time on his side, he decided to wait. He didn't know why. It was just one of those feelings he got every now and then. About the time he had convinced himself to move a little closer, he heard the guard. It was the muffled snort of a snoring man. Reed moved without a sound to the back of the first tree.

He looked around the tree and found the warrior leaning back against it. He was sleeping soundly and Reed planned for him to never wake up. He took his knife in his right hand and without thinking plunged it into his chest while at the same time he pinned his head to the tree with his left hand as it covered his mouth. The Indian never knew a thing and didn't make a sound. Reed held him and twisted the knife while death moved into his body. He was a young man. That didn't bother Reed because he was also an Apache warrior. Given the same opportunity, he would have killed Haddok without thinking about it. Reed felt no remorse. He never looked at killing a man as his first choice. He hoped he would always look for a way to let any man live. In this case, there were seven of them and one of him. He had no other choice. They were holding the man who saved his life and he intended to get him out of there. He did not plan on talking to anybody or walking around them. He would do what it took to get Tall Tree home.

He wiped his knife on the ground and took the blanket the warrior had wrapped around him. He threw it around his shoulders and walked slowly toward the camp. He decided to change his plans and take the warriors around the fire before he got the other guard. If for some reason they decided to change the guards before he got through, then he would have to deal with the other five while they were awake. They would find the dead guard and sound the alarm. His element of surprise would be lost and his job a lot harder.

He tried to look like one of them as he walked up to the camp. He pulled the blanket up around his face as if he was cold. He stopped at the edge of the flickering light and took a look at the exact positions of the five warriors. They were all rolled up in their blankets close to the fire. It was a chilly night and the fire must have felt good to them.

He held his knife in his right hand beneath the blanket while he held it closed with his left. He was about to move into the circle when one of them set straight up and looked around. He grunted a few words that Reed didn't understand and then rolled over and stood up. He started walking toward Haddok. Reed turned his back to the Indian in a quick movement and stood still. He walked by Reed on his left and on toward the stream. Reed followed. He was going to relieve himself.

Suddenly realization hit the warrior. He probably realized all the people who were supposed to be in camp were back there sleeping. He whirled around to face Reed and Haddok's knife went in just below the rib cage. He pushed it up and raised the warrior off the ground. His left hand covered the man's mouth while his body went limp. Reed lowered him to the ground quietly. He was dead even before Reed started to lay him down. He wiped the blood off his knife again and stood to wrap the blanket back around him. He faced the camp. There was no movement.

He walked back to the fire and did not stop to think or look around. The first one he killed by kneeling down alongside the warrior's sleeping body and pushing the knife through his blanket. He covered the warrior's mouth and muffled the groan that came from his throat. He quickly went to the second and did him the same way. The third was on his back and Reed covered his mouth as he slit his throat. The last one was curled up with his back to Reed. He knelt behind him and thrust the knife into his back. All four were dead in a matter of three or four minutes.

Reed turned to look at his friend. The fire light reflected off Tall Tree's eyes. He was looking right at Reed. He said nothing and Reed did not go to him. He wanted to, but he had one more to take care of. Reed didn't think Tall Tree had a clue who he was. He only knew somebody was killing the Apaches. He probably thought he would be next. Reed stood and walked out of the camp toward where he figured the last warrior would be.

He headed up the high ground. Reed decided he would just walk up on this one. The guard would think it was someone coming to spell him. Reed wasn't sure where he was so he needed the warrior's help. Haddok faked a cough and made plenty of noise walking. Sure enough, a voice spoke out. Reed didn't respond. He just kept going. The warrior stepped out in front of him and said something. Reed walked right to him and the knife came up out of the blanket and caught him in the chest. Haddok pushed it upwards real hard and felt the life leave him. He left him where he fell and walked back to the camp as fast as he could.

He walked over to Tall Tree. If the wounded Indian was afraid, he didn't show it. His eyes were focused on the mystery man and a slight sign of puzzlement was in them. As Reed knelt down in front of him he let the blanket fall to the ground. A smile broke across Haddok's face.

"I've come to get you and take you home, my friend," Reed spoke softly.

"How did you know to look for me?" he asked.

"We'll talk about that later. I've got to get you out of here." Haddok was untying Tall Tree's hands as he spoke.

"We must hurry. The ones who left are bringing back other warriors to show off their captive," he said. "It would be better for you to leave. I cannot help you. I have lost a lot of blood and my leg is so bad I cannot walk."

"I will not leave you. I made a promise to Shining Moon I plan on keeping." He was more puzzled by what Reed said. Before Tall Tree could speak, Reed continued, "I will get you out of here just like you got me out of my mess. I'll carry you all the way to hell and back if I have to. You just lay still for a little while. I've got some work to do."

Reed took the leather strips the Apaches had used to tie Tall Tree's hands and tied them back just like he found them. He moved over to the dead Indians and repositioned their bodies so they were lying face up. He folded their arms across their chests and covered them with blankets. He then retrieved his clothes and came back dressed and ready. He brushed out all the sign of his presence around the camp and went to kneel in front of Tall Tree. The big Indian had quietly been watching it all.

"What are you doing?" Tall Tree asked.

"I'm just playing with their minds a bit. The time I spent might give us a couple of hours. They'l talk a while trying to figure out what happened and what it means."

"I do that at times too," he answered with a smile.

20

"Here's my plan," Reed told Tall Tree. "They will think you took the stream to leave. I'm hoping they will think you got loose and killed their brothers. If so, they will move slowly. They know how bad you were injured and the mystery of it all will make them cautious. I'm going to carry you out over the mountain. I need your help. If I can get you to a place where we can hole up for a spell, then I'll come back and take them on a long trail. What we need is a concealed place with some water. Do you know of such a place?"

"I do. It is a half day walk for me from this place. It will take you more carrying me."

"That's good. I don't know how much time we've got before the others return. We better get moving. Do you need me to do anything for your leg before we head out?"

"No. They stopped the bleeding. I need a drink of water before we start."

Reed fetched him some water and Tall Tree drank it in long sips.

"How do we get to this place?" Reed asked.

"At the top of this mountain," he pointed behind him, "there is a trail that runs down the other side about halfway and then turns north. It follows that direction for a while and then drops down to the valley. The trail turns at a small stream running off the mountain. Follow that stream down to the valley and cross it where the stream turns south. The trail leads up another mountain. When on top, it turns north again. You will come to a steep rock wall. Follow the wall to the right. A few hundred paces along the wall you will find a big cedar that appears to be growing out of the wall. Behind the trunk of the tree there is a small crack you can squeeze through. It opens to a wider place after a few steps and there you will find a hole in the rock with a small pool of water. I have slept there many nights."

Reed looked his friend square in the eye and spoke with certainty, "This ain't going to be easy for you, but we will make it."

Reed lifted Tall Tree so he could stand on his good leg. He bent over and placed his shoulder against the Indian's belly and lifted him. Tall Tree lowered his head and shoulders down Reed's back. Reed was careful with his leg as he shifted the big man for comfort.

"They took the knife you gave me. I want it," Tall Tree spoke from Reed's back.

"I've got it in my belt. Let's get out of here."

21

The Rocking H ranch.

Josh Spencer stood leaning against the pole fence while his cowhands worked the horses. They were separating some young ones from their mamas. He planned to keep the best and sell the rest. They had a couple of good stallions on the ranch and were producing some fine stock. Josh couldn't remember when he wasn't on top of a horse and he loved this part of his work more than anything.

One of the cowhands interrupted Josh's enjoyment by yelling and pointing toward the north. Josh turned and saw another of his men riding toward them leading two horses. He immediately recognized Bud's horse and walked out to meet Jake Baldwin as he rode up. The other hands stopped what they were doing and followed.

Jake had gone out early in the morning to check on some cattle on the north range. He pulled up and stepped down. "I found them heading this way a couple of miles out. Something must have happened to Reed."

The cowhands started clabbering how they were going to saddle up and go get whoever shot their boss.

Josh was looking the horse over. He turned grinning, "That ain't necessary. You won't find Reed. I've tried to find him a bunch of times and I ain't done it yet. Nearly did one time, but he knew I was there long before I knew where he was."

"But he may be out there hurt," one of the men exclaimed.

"I don't think so. His rifle is in its case and his boots and hat are tied to the saddle. I ain't met the man who could take any of the three away from him. I know Bud Haddok pretty well. I don't know what he's up to, but whatever it is, these horses and gear were in his way. He's doing some foot work and he knew the horses would find their way home."

"He'll need a ride," Jake said. "Maybe we ought to ride out that way."

"Naw. I'll give him a couple of days and then I'll ride out to a place where he can come and find me when he's ready. Ya'll get back to work and I'll put the horses up."

As Josh stripped the horses, he thought, you be careful Bud. I plan on you standing up with me when I get married.

22

Reed carried his friend for about a half hour before he stopped to rest. He was still not back to his full strength and carrying Tall Tree was a clear reminder. Tall Tree was the biggest Indian Reed had ever seen. He was a good two inches taller than Reed and probably weighed twenty-five pounds more. Tall Tree was taking the uncomfortable ride real good. He said nothing while Reed was walking. When Reed stopped to rest, he lowered Tall Tree to a waist high flat rock.

"You are a good man," Tall Tree said. "You risk your life for me. I have never had that."

"It wasn't no risk," Reed said with a smile. "You had'em so worn out it was easy."

Tall Tree smiled back. "The ones who left went to their main village. They spoke that they would be back by dark tomorrow. We have time, but we need to get to the place I spoke of before the sun rises. It will be hot when the sun shines."

"As long as you can hold out, we'll be fine. I'll need you to help me find the place in the dark."

"My head hanging down makes it hard. I am fighting to stay awake," he said.

"Well, I've caught my breath. We better get going," Reed said. He stood Tall Tree up and lifted him to his shoulder. He still had some climbing to do. It ought to be a little easier when up on top.

Reed did his best to stay on the rocky ground, but it made walking harder. He was trying to leave as little sign as possible.

The next rest came when Reed topped out on the mountain. He needed it. He was sucking wind in long gasps when he lowered Tall Tree to the ground. Reed laid down on his back and didn't say anything for a spell. He couldn't.

Tall Tree broke the silence. His voice seemed weaker. "The trail stays on top for a while before it goes halfway down. There is a big rock that will block your path. It goes down at the rock. It will then turn when you get to the tall trees."

"I'll find the way. You just hang on. You have to make it. I promised your wife."

"We must talk about that. How did you speak to Shining Moon?"

"We'll talk about it later. I think I have enough air in me to get going," Reed said.

He loaded him up and started out. It was a lot easier walking on fairly even ground. Reed was not sure he could have done much more climbing.

They rested again at the rock where the trail turned. Tall Tree was semi-conscious. He mumbled some in his language. The rest was short. The next part was downhill and Reed figured it would be as hard as climbing. However, he made it fine and turned north at the tree line. He didn't stop again until he reached the trickle of water that marked the next turn in the trail.

He lowered Tall Tree and fell down with his face in the water.

He drank a belly full and then cupped some in his hands to give to Tall Tree. The water roused him a bit and he drank as Reed lifted it repeatedly. Reed poured some over Tall Tree's face. He then went back to drink again. Reed judged it to be about midnight. They rested about a half hour, drank again, and headed out.

The walking was easier now and Reed made good time. They reached the stream at the valley floor two hours later. They both drank again.

"We cross a short distance up stream. It is easier there," Tall Tree said. "When you cross, go up the stream until you see the mountains on both sides of the water. The trail turns up the mountain where the water makes a turn. It will lead you to the rock wall I spoke of."

"We are going to make it Tall Tree. Don't you quit on me," Reed said. He lifted the Indian and walked on.

He came to the rock wall about an hour later and turned right at it's base. A short time later he saw the big cedar. He put Tall Tree down and moved up to check it out. He found the break in the wall behind the thick growth of the tree. He went back and brought Tall Tree to the place and stood him on his good leg. He hopped him over to the entrance. Reed squeezed through and helped Tall Tree to follow. It was tight.

After a few steps it became wider and a little further on they came to the hole back on one side. It was a perfect natural shelter. A small pool of water, fed by a trickle from the rocks, was on one side. They both lay down to drink. Then came the exhausted deep sleep.

23

Haddok woke up three times before light. Each time he listened and heard nothing. Tall Tree slept soundly. Reed felt of him each time he awoke and he was warm, but not with fever. Reed had not looked at his wounds, but there was no fresh bleeding.

Reed woke the final time and it was getting light enough for him to see. The place they were in was a natural cut in the rock wall. The space allowing their entrance was a shift in the upper surface from long ago. Looking up he saw the cut was about four feet across all the way to the top. It looked about forty feet straight up with sheer walls on both sides. It played out as the cut narrowed about twenty feet beyond their shelter. As long as they stayed still and the Apaches didn't find the entrance, he felt safe. If they found the entrance, then it would take thirty-one Apaches to get to them because he didn't have but thirty shells for his pistol. He could hold off an army in there.

He cupped some water in his hands and slid over to give it to Tall Tree. It woke him.

"You are a strong man, Haddok. That is your name?"

"Yes. Shining Moon told me your name is Tall Tree."

"Tell me how you talked with Shining Moon?" Tall Tree asked.

"I came two nights ago to bring you more gifts. It was dark when I placed them in your valley. I was leaving when Shining Moon met me in the brush beside the stream. She told me you left on a hunt that morning and shortly after you left the valley, a party of Apaches crossed the stream below the waterfall. Your guard later heard a rifle shot. She was worried you had been killed or wounded. She told me you would die before you would lead the Apaches to your village. She spoke of your law. She told me you broke the law when you brought me to your valley. She said you did it because you felt it right to save a brave man's life."

"So Shining Moon broke the law and came outside to speak with you." Tall Tree had a stern look.

"Yes. She said you are a brave man. She asked me to find you and help you."

Tall Tree thought for a moment and then a slight smile entered the corners of his mouth. "There is no law that would keep Shining Moon from helping me. I am not surprised."

"I made her a promise and I'm gonna keep it," Haddok replied. "We've got some big problems to deal with. For one, there's no telling how many Apaches we have on our tail. The biggest problem is we don't have any food or medicine for your wound. Another problem is I've got to get you home before I get so weak I can't carry you. Lay out for me where we are in relation to your valley and tell me how we get there."

"Our valley is like this," Tall Tree said as he wet a finger in his mouth and drew a circle on the rock floor. "The waterfall is here." He marked the south part of the circle. "We are here," he said, marking a line of mountains to the east of their valley. "There is no mountain between us. We are next to our valley."

"How far is it around your valley?"

"I have walked all the way around it in half a day."

"I think what I need to do is go back and remove as much sign as I can. At the place where we crossed the stream I will leave clear sign that goes south. After I've led them that way a spell I'll dump them in some spot where they'll have to work to trail me. I'll then double back, get you, and we'll go all the way around the north end of your valley. We'll come to the waterfall from the west." Haddok was using his method of a wet finger to explain.

"It is a good plan. Let me tell you of something you can use. Apaches are very superstitious. I was given a name by my village when I was a boy. The name is He Who Runs With Spirits. My people call me Ghost Runner. The Apaches know that name and it is why I would be a prized captive. Anything you do to cause them to wonder will slow them down. You did the right thing when you did not cut the cords that tied me. By tying their knots back, you left it so they could think I got loose and killed their brothers."

"That's what I wanted to do. Ghost Runner, huh. I may have to sleep somewhere else tonight," Reed said with a laugh.

"The Apaches are good trackers. Hiding our trail will be hard."

"I know they will eventually work it out. I just want to buy us some time so I can get you home."

They talked on a little while. When Tall Tree started trying to thank him Reed left.

24

It was mid-afternoon when Blue Dog led the Apaches into the camp. His chief Spotted Horse and the tribal elders had willingly come with him. The news of the capture of He Who Runs With Spirits had spread quickly through their village and they had left immediately.

But their excitement was soured as they looked around. The camp looked like a burial ground. Flies were swarming the blood soaked blankets covering their brothers. One warrior dismounted and pulled back one blanket after another. The dead were all blankly staring up with folded arms.

Spotted Horse turned to Blue Dog. "Where is He Who Runs With Spirits?" he asked angrily.

"He was tied to that tree," Blue Dog replied, pointing to the small tree where they had left him.

Two warriors bounded off their horses and ran to the tree. One of them exclaimed, "The leather that held him has not been cut or loosened. It is as if he just removed his wrists from it."

A murmur went through the warriors and their horses began to move around nervously, sensing the tension of those who sat their backs.

"This cannot be," Blue Dog said. "I saw him tied and he was tied well. He was also injured so badly I thought he might die. Our warriors had to carry him here. He could not have done what you think."

"Look about," Spotted Horse ordered. "See if there is any sign that someone helped him."

The warriors fanned out like ants. Some dismounted and moved about over the area. Others rode out a short distance circling the camp while they searched the ground. Spotted Horse, Blue Dog, and a few of the older men sat on their horses and contemplated the scene.

Spotted Horse said to Blue Dog, "You left young warriors here to guard a man we have at times thought was a Spirit. The young men are now dead from knife wounds. Whoever held the knife knew how to kill. Answer me! How did he kill all of them? If he was wounded as bad as you say, how did he do it? Answer me."

"I cannot answer you," Blue Dog said, looking shamefully at the ground.

"If we find sign he had help, then I will understand. If we find no sign, then it will prove he is not a real man," Spotted Horse responded.

Blue Dog mustered some nerve and said, "Our people who saw him long ago swear he is a man. When the warriors brought him here, he looked like a man. Yes he is larger than any Indian in our village, but do spirits bleed? He was bleeding badly and I had the men put medicine on his wounds to stop it."

"It is said that spirits can look like men. It may be he wanted to be found and brought to your camp so he could kill Apaches," Spotted Horse answered.

As they talked, Blue Dog became less certain about He Who Runs With Spirits. The warriors checking the area came back a few at a time declaring they could find no sign he had help. The warriors were huddled and nervously eying the dead warriors, looking about as if they expected to be killed by some mysterious man at any moment.

"If he had help, they would have gone to the water to leave no trail," Spotted Horse said. "Search both sides until you find a trail we can follow. Some of you take the mountain and look for tracks. Two of you put the dead men on their horses and return them to our village. Let me know when you have found a trail." He was unsure of what happened here. There had to be some sign. The Apaches followed his orders and left Spotted Horse, Blue Dog, and two others at the camp.

Spotted Horse directed his attention to Blue Dog. "Blue Dog, you know the families of the young warriors who died here will hold you responsible. I hope we can find He Who Runs With Spirits."

"We will find him. He cannot go far with his wounds," Blue Dog said.

"I would think he could not kill seven warriors with his wounds. It will be good if we find he had help," Spotted Horse continued.

"If he had no help, I am not sure we want to find him. The spirit he runs with would be too strong for us," Blue Dog said.

"Even you are now beginning to doubt that he is a real man," Spotted Horse said.

"I know I saw him and touched him. I cannot explain what has happened here."

They talked and waited. An hour passed with nothing found.

Suddenly a warrior raced into the camp from the mountain and declared, "We have found his sign up on the mountain. The trail is hard to see, but we can follow."

"Go get the ones along the stream and return here. We will all follow the trail. Is it the tracks of one man?" Spotted Horse questioned.

"There is only the sign of one man."

They waited until the warriors returned to the camp and they all headed up the mountain.

25

Haddok left the hideout in the early light and backtracked to the stream crossing. He erased all the sign he could as he traveled. He found plenty of his own sign at the stream. He tried to get rid of it.

He then headed south along the stream leaving clear footprints on the bank. He walked a long way hoping the Apaches would get all worked up over the clear trail. Eventually he dropped off into the stream and continued to follow the flow for about an hour. Reed was on the lookout for just the right place to leave the stream. He checked out a couple of places that didn't work out. Then he saw it.

In front of him was a low limb reaching out over the water a good ten feet. Directly across the stream from the limb was a rock shelf reaching down toward the bank, ending about six feet from the water.

Haddok moved across the stream to the western bank and stepped out onto the soft bank. He left clear footprints away from the water until he was walking on rock. He then made his way on the rock surface back to the stream. When he came to the shelf reaching down to the water, he got a running start and jumped as far as he could out into the stream.

He got fairly wet, but it felt good. He moved over under the overhanging limb and pulled himself up out of the water. He slid along on the limb until he came to the tree trunk, swung around it, and followed another low limb out to drop to the ground fifteen feet away from the tree. He headed up the mountain and when he got to the top he turned back north.

It was close to noon when he reached the high ground above the stream crossing where he started his ruse earlier in the day. He was slipping along quietly, fully aware that he could encounter the Apaches at any time.

Reed's thoughts went to his belly. He tried to remember when he had eaten last. Except for a few pieces of jerked beef, it had been nearly three days. He knew full well because his belly kept talking to him. He suddenly froze in his tracks. What was the sound he just heard? He stood very still and listened. It was the sound of horses jumping into the stream down below. He heard a shrill yell. They were at the crossing. They were moving much too fast for him to keep ahead of them unless they took the bait and followed his tracks south.

He left out at a fast clip without knowing. He had to get back to Tall Tree and start moving toward his valley.

26

The Apaches reached the stream crossing about noon. Working the trail out was slow for a while. They now were making good time. They splashed across the stream and were confronted with clear mocassin clad footprints leading south.

"Look at the tracks of your wounded man, Blue Dog," Spotted Horse said loud enough for all the warriors to hear. "Near death and cannot walk. You expect us to believe these are the tracks of a wounded man? His steps are long and strong. He is not dragging a leg." Spotted Horse seemed to be enjoying the humiliation of Blue Dog.

Blue Dog hung his head in sulking despair and wondered what had gone wrong. He planned to be the talk of bravery around their campfires this winter. He should have stayed with He Who Runs With Spirits and sent the others with the news. He chose not to respond to Spotted Horse. There was nothing to say.

"Follow his tracks," ordered Spotted Horse. "They are fresh and we are gaining."

They followed the clear trail until it entered the water. Then they covered both sides and went downstream. They went past the place where Haddok left the water because the men on the west bank were moving slower. When they came up on the footprints leaving the water, one of them let out a yelp. The others raced back and the band sat their horses in the water looking at the tracks.

"He left the water here," a warrior on foot said.

"Yes. He is going this way," another said, pointing west.

"Follow him. We are getting close," Spotted Horse responded.

They followed to find no trail at all. The prints died out when they came to the rock surface. They moved back and forth in a westerly direction for about two hours. They found no sign.

"We have lost him. We will go back to the water and look again," Spotted Horse said.

It was getting late when they reached the stream and the shadows were swallowing the stream before their eyes. They began to search the area around the footprints again. One warrior went to the other side and got down on his hands and knees to comb the ground. His eyes focused on something and he raised himself and shouted, "He came this way."

They rushed to him and he stopped them. "There has been no wind. I found three small green twigs from this tree on the ground. He came out of the water on the limb," the warrior said pointing to the overhanging limb. "He dropped down over here to go up the mountain."

Spotted Horse smiled and said, "He Who Runs With Spirits is not Apache. He cannot fool us." He sat on his horse and pondered for a moment. "It will be dark soon. We must not lose his trail. We will make camp here and trail him when it is light. Build your fires big and stay close to them. No warrior will stand guard alone. Half of us will sleep first. Then we will change so the others can sleep. Tie the horses in close so you can watch them."

They carried out their chief's orders and soon fires were burning and tired warriors were rolling into blankets. Those staying awake were quiet and alert. Their look gave away the feeling that was also flooding the minds of those trying to sleep. They were on an uncertain journey and not sure what might happen when and if they caught up to He Who Runs With Spirits. To a man they hoped someone else would be the first to come face to face with him.

27

Haddok returned to the hiding place and found Tall Tree sleeping. The big Indian was getting weaker. He felt weaker than a piece of straw himself. The Apaches were close. If they took the bait and followed the false trail, it wouldn't take them long to work it out. They were good. His only hope was to get Tall Tree back to his village.

"The Apaches are hot on our trail," Reed said as he shook Tall Tree awake. "I tried to buy us a little time. If it don't work, we don't have any time at all."

"Leave me here and save yourself," Tall Tree said.

"We are going together and we are going to make it." Reed was trying to convince himself as much as Tall Tree.

He helped Tall Tree up and hopped him to the entrance. He then went out and led him through. He lifted him to his shoulder and started north around the sheer rock wall. He stopped often to rest. It was hard to get going again after each stop. The rocky floor made walking slow and tough.

It got dark quick and Reed sat Tall Tree in some boulders and went back down the trail to see if the Apaches were close. He didn't think they would continue after dark and he was hoping to see a campfire. If he could, then he would go to them and mess up their night a bit. He saw no sign of them. They had taken the bait. Even with that, he realized he would be lucky to get all the way around the valley and into the entrance before they caught up.

He went back to Tall Tree, lifted him, and started out again. The going was so tough in the rocks he had to shuffle along feeling his way. If he fell, it would surely start Tall Tree's leg to bleeding. He wouldn't live long if it did.

The next time he stopped, Tall Tree spoke. "We have come to a place where you can walk away from the wall and into the trees. The ground is level there and the walking is easier."

Reed took him at his word and sure enough he made a lot better time. It bothered him some because he would be leaving more sign. The Apaches were getting so close that sign didn't matter much any more. He figured the Apaches would split when they came to the rock wall. Whatever they did, he fully expected to deal with them before the next day passed. He didn't know what he would do when the time came.

Sometime in the early morning hours Reed heard the sound of a stream. He made his way to it and laid Tall Tree on the ground. He cupped water and gave it to him. He drank all he could hold himself. He splashed water on his face and it felt good. Tall Tree fell asleep before Reed finished drinking. Reed lay down beside him to rest a little and did not know when he drifted off.

Reed was shocked when the warmth of the sun startled him awake. Tall Tree was still sleeping. Reed looked for the sun trying to figure how late in the morning it was. He couldn't tell. He knew for sure he had slept away some valuable time.

He stood and walked back down the trail a spell to check it out. He stopped in some thick brush where he could see a good distance.

He saw the first Apache when he came out from the rock wall. He was afoot and looking at the ground for sign. Reed didn't see the rest of them. He didn't have to. He knew they would be close behind. He hightailed it back to Tall Tree and woke him. He lifted the Indian to his shoulder and headed out down the stream bank.

He was headed straight toward the rock wall. If he could get there and hunker down in some rocks, he might be able to hold them off and reduce the odds a bit. He wouldn't have to worry about them slipping up behind him. He had to get to that wall.

28

Reed was walking as fast as he could. He came to a sudden stop when a loud sound flooded his ears. He had never heard anything like it before. It was a sucking sound. He lowered Tall Tree to the ground and asked, "What is that?"

"It is where the water hides," Tall Tree explained.

"What do you mean?"

"The stream we follow is the one that runs through our valley. It runs into the ground at the base of the mountain that surrounds our valley."

"You mean the entire stream just disappears?"

"Yes. It falls into a hole right up against the mountain."

"Have you found where it comes out of the mountain in your valley?"

"I've been there many times. It runs out of the side of the mountain down at the ground."

"Is there any space at the top of the hole the water runs through?"

"Most of the time there is. When the rains come, the hole is full."

"Have you ever tried to go up in the hole from your side?"

"Yes. We cannot go far. The water flows so swift."

"Let's get up there to it. It may be our only chance. There's no way we are going to outrun them. I'd rather die on my own terms than let them kill me."

Reed picked Tall Tree up and moved toward the sound. He came to the place where the water rushed headlong into the ground. He placed Tall Tree down and stood looking at the marvel of nature. An entire strong mountain stream, over thirty feet across, just disappeared into the ground. He got close enough to look down into the hole and it looked like the water fell about fifty feet before it bounced off the rock bottom and shot into the side of the mountain.

"How far is it across this mountain?" Reed asked Tall Tree.

"I do not know. I have been up there, but I have never counted the steps."

Reed quickly looked around the bank and found what he needed. It was a log washed up on the bank from some long ago rain storm. It was about ten feet long and a good thirty inches in diameter. It was dry and not so heavy. Reed dragged it to the bank just above the hole. He came back to Tall Tree and took some of his leather strips. He tied one around the middle of the log. He then fashioned two loops from another strip and tied it to the first.

"How long can you hold your breath?" he asked Tall Tree.

"I do not know."

"I don't know either. We're just going to have to hold it as long as it takes."

Reed helped Tall Tree over by the log and explained, "We are going to put one of our wrists into the loops to keep us with the log. I hope the log will cushion the blows to the rocks below. I also hope it will float us to the surface once we get inside the tunnel. I'm counting on enough space at the surface for us to breathe. If there ain't no air space, then we're goners. There's no way we can hold our breath that long."

"It is good. The Apaches will not get to have fun with us before we die," Tall Tree said with a smile.

Reed pushed the log out into the water with enough of it still on the bank for him to control it. He helped Tall Tree down into the water. Tall Tree braced against the swift stream with his good leg. Tall Tree put his wrist through the loop and pulled it tight. He was facing downstream. Reed climbed in on the other side of the log and thrust his wrist into the loop and tightened it. He braced his legs and leaned into the current. He then pulled the log all the way into the water. It was all he could do to keep the log and Tall Tree from spilling over into the hole.

Reed was looking over Tall Tree's shoulder at the spot where he figured the Apaches would come into sight. Tall Tree looked across the log at him and said, "Haddok, you are a brave man. It is good for me to know you. I will take you with me wherever I go."

"The same goes for me. I'm proud to call you friend."

Reed was looking into his eyes when he heard the Apaches shout and heard shots ring out. Water splashed near them and he heard the zing of bullets. He ducked his head low, lifted his legs, and the current took them over the edge and down into the swirling storm of water.

29

As they went over the edge Reed tried to twist the log so one end would hit the bottom first. He could just see them being smacked against the rocks. He couldn't get the log turned. The water took charge and they were along for the ride.

Reed looked through the cascade and was amazed at how calm Tall Tree was. Reed tried to brace himself for the lick that was coming. At the same time he was trying to gage when he should draw the last big breath.

At that moment they were jerked up toward the surface. It was a fierce change of direction. The log quickly became their enemy. It beat their bodies and they could not get away from it. It bounced around in the water like a twig.

On their way up, there was another swift change of direction as they were swept like lightning to one side and down again. Reed sucked in one long gasp of air and held on tight. They were bouncing off rock walls, rolling and tumbling in a dark world. Reed feared being pushed up against a boulder or turn and being held there by the force of the water. It relieved him somewhat to feel the fast current moving them. If they were to get to an air pocket, they needed to do it fast.

Reed tried to be calm. He determined to hold his breath. Some of the blows against the walls had knocked a little of the wind out of him. He locked every muscle in his body and willed himself not to breathe.

Then the rapid movement seemed to slow a bit and Reed tried to make out anything he could in the dark water. He felt Tall Tree's body hit up against his throughout the ordeal. He could not see him even though he was only inches away.

Suddenly the flow became smooth and he felt the log fighting its way upward. He followed and felt it when it bumped the rock surface. He jammed his face up and felt the cool damp air. His lungs were crying out for help and he gulped the fresh air deep inside with grunts of desperation. He could hear Tall Tree doing the same. They were alive.

He felt the top of the tunnel and found about six inches of air space. They were still moving smoothly in the water. He was about to speak to Tall Tree when the air space disappeared. He was able to draw in a little air before they went back under.

Haddok usually never panicked in tough situations, but he was close to doing so. He didn't have enough air in his lungs to last long. He couldn't get a hold on this thing so he could whip it. Matter of fact, it had a hold on him and he couldn't get loose.

After what seemed like an eternity, they bobbed up again. This time there was about a foot of air space and both men gulped in air and groaned like two babies. It was still completely dark. They learned from the first experience and both were breathing deep and trying to get ready for another trip under the water. It never came. They flowed smoothly along with the current.

"How are you doing?" Reed asked.

"The pain is all over me," he replied.

"Me too. Hang on. We are going to ride this thing through."

Reed barely got the words out of his mouth before seeing a faint light reflecting off the water in front of them. "Look! Look there! I see some light," he cried.

"I see it. We are going to make it through."

They held onto the log and let the current do the work as they moved toward the light. It seemed to take forever. The light became brighter until the stream spit them out of the dark hole into brilliant sunlight.

They slowly guided themselves to the eastern bank. Reed pulled his knife, cut the leather, and let the log ride on. He helped Tall Tree up on the bank and both fell to the ground exhausted. Tall Tree reached over and grasped Reed's arm and squeezed. The squeeze spoke a thousand words. Like two panting dogs, they lay breathing clean air and letting the sun warm their cold bodies. Reed looked at his friend and to his surprise found him sleeping. It seemed so crazy. One minute he was being tossed around like a leaf in a cyclone and the next he was sleeping like a newborn calf. Somewhere in the amazement, Reed too shut his eyes and fell into the deep sleep of exhaustion.

30

Spotted Horse's band had gained on He Who Runs With Spirits. When they came to the rock wall they split their party and planned to meet where the trail left the wall. He went with the warriors heading north. They soon found sign and picked up the pace. The trail moved away from the wall and the sign was clear. They moved fast and rode out on the bank of the stream to see He Who Runs With Spirits out in the water. He was holding on to a log.

They began firing at their enemy. Suddenly one end of the log shot up in the air. The log and the man disappeared. They kicked their horses into a run and raced to the spot. The sound shocked them and they pulled up gazing at the sight of the entire stream pouring into the earth in a swirling frenzy.

They looked at it from horseback for a moment and then dismounted to walk closer. The earth had swallowed the water and He Who Runs With Spirits.

"Could it be this man's spirits have come and rescued him," a warrior said.

"That cannot be," Blue Dog said. "The water has done our

job. He Who Runs With Spirits died here this day. Our names will be great through the land." He said it as if he was trying to convince them of something he was uncertain about himself.

The entire band of warriors stood dumbfounded. Never having seen this place before, the stream's disappearance was beyond their understanding. To them, the hole had suddenly come and taken He Who Runs With Spirits right before their eyes.

Spotted Horse spoke. "I do not know what has happened here. We cannot go back and tell this without knowing. Who will go into the hole and find out?" Spotted Horse was a brave man. He knew he would not go into the hole. He did not expect his warriors to go. He asked the question to put more shame on Blue Dog. If anyone should go, it would be him.

They looked at each other with a mixture of fear and unwillingness. Blue Dog did not let his eyes make contact with any of them.

"We will camp here and wait. We will wait until we know. We must be able to say if He Who Runs With Spirits is alive or dead," Spotted Horse said.

They moved away from the hole and began to make camp. They left a guard at the hole. They soon had a fire going and were nervously settling in to wait. The other half of the Apaches rode up to their camp before dark. They heard the story and looked into the hole. When dark came, they had three fires burning high and all the warriors were in close.

31

After they woke up, Haddok and Tall Tree sat soaking up the warmth of the sun. Haddok's body was trembling even though the sun was warm. Part of the reason was the cold water he had been in and the other part was he had walked up to death during the ordeal and looked him straight in the eye. He hadn't seen any quit in him and knew he was one lucky man. It's a fearsome thing to be at the mercy of something you have no control over. Reed rolled the dice and they came up smiling. He was proud.

He looked over at Tall Tree and said, "Let's get you home."

"Follow the stream," he muttered.

Reed stood and stretched his sore muscles. Every part of his body was hurting. He helped Tall Tree to his good leg and lifted him. He started out thinking, it is good to be walking.

He walked for about thirty minutes and the valley suddenly opened before him. He moved away from the stream and started across a large grassy field. He was halfway across when he saw an Indian standing in the tree line in front of him. The Indian disappeared about the time he saw him.

Reed kept walking and when he came to the spot where he

saw the Indian he heard a commotion in the woods. There must have been fifteen Indians in the group rushing toward him, men and women. He lowered Tall Tree to the ground as they ran up.

"I knew you would find him," Shining Moon said. How did you get into the valley?"

"We came through the hole in the mountain where the stream flows," Reed answered.

"I cannot believe this. It is impossible. The Spirit surely was with you."

"Yes mam', I reckon he was. Tall Tree is in bad shape. He has a gunshot wound to his leg. I have not had time to touch it. The only doctoring he's had is what the Apaches did. They captured him and I took him from them. They were hot on our trail when we went into the water on the other side of the mountain."

"We heard their rifles. We will take you to our village. You have the look of one who needs medicine too."

Some of the men lifted Tall Tree and two of the men took Reed's arms and draped them around their necks to help him walk. He did not know how tired he really was til then. His legs were dragging most of the time.

Upon their arrival the women got to work on both of them. Shining moon was tending Tall Tree and two young women removed Reed's shirt and pants. He didn't put up any fight. He didn't have any left in him. They bathed his scrapes and cuts. Then they rubbed them with a greasy substance that felt cool and soothing. He was covered with a blanket while someone took his clothes to the stream to wash them. A pot of steaming soup was brought to him and he sipped it a bit. It tasted good. As it cooled, he began to drink it in gulps. When empty, one of the women refilled the pot. After finishing off the second pot, Reed laid back on the soft ground and fell into a deep sleep.

It was still light when he roused up. He focused his eyes and turned to look around. He was shocked to see what he figured to be everybody in the village seated around him watching him sleep. Tall Tree was leaning back against a small sapling with his eyes fixed on Haddok.

"Haddok, will you sleep forever?" Tall Tree said with a smile.

"I believe I could. How are you feeling?"

"I am better. I am home and Shining Moon's medicine is good."

Shining Moon spoke. "Tall Tree told us all you did for him. We all know you are a brave man. We will hold you in our hearts."

"No mam', I'm not brave. It is an honor to help Tall Tree. I will always owe him for my life."

"Perhaps it is good for two brave men to owe each other so much," she said.

"I reckon so," Reed said as he looked over to the big man he carried on his shoulder for two days.

"It is true," Tall Tree said.

32

Haddok and the Indians of the village sat and talked for a while. Tall Tree introduced his daughters Pale moon and Morning Light. They were the beautiful women who had tended to him earlier. He then introduced his son, Tree Wind. Reed would have known him as Tall Tree's son. He had his father's look and large frame.

"What kind of Indian are you?" Reed asked Tall Tree.

"We are Moqui. Our people were here long before the others. Some now are known as Hopi. We keep the ancient name. The ancient ones, the Anasazi, are our forefathers."

"I've never heard of the Moqui tribe."

"We are not many. The Apache and Navajo raid our villages. They kill many and take captives. This is why we live here in our secret place."

The talk went on. Reed shared about his family back in Texas and the strong love he had for his father and sister. He told them of Samantha and their plans to be married.

"I would like to meet such a woman that could be the wife of Haddok," Tall Tree said. All those seated around laughed. "I have a strong wife. Shining moon was born Apache. She is now Moqui." They all smiled at this, especially Shining Moon.

The talk was interrupted by a Moqui warrior running into their circle. "The Apaches camp where the water hides. I climbed to look."

"We must be quiet. They will look everywhere for me," Tall Tree said.

"I have an idea that sure would be fun," Reed broke in.

"What would Haddok be thinking for our enemies?" Tall Tree asked.

Reed looked at Tree Wind and asked, "Could you teach me to shoot a bow real quick?"

"It is not hard," Tree Wind replied.

"Then fetch me a bow and arrows," Reed said.

"I do not understand fetch," Tree Wind said with a puzzled look.

"It means bring them to me," Reed explained.

Tree Wind jumped up and was back in no time with a bow and a fist full of arrows.

Reed turned to Shining Moon and inquired, "Since you came from the Apaches, do you still use their language?"

"Yes."

"Could you teach me to say He Who Runs With Spirits in Apache?"

She smiled as if she knew what Reed was up to and said, "Hikeel wix Thiidn." She dragged it out to make it sound eerie.

Reed listened to her and it sounded like she said, "High kill wax the den." He mulled the words in his mind and spit out, in a ghostly voice, "Hiii killll waxxx theeeeee den."

"You sound like Apache," she complimented.

Reed practiced saying the words over and over until he had it down. Then he turned to Tree Wind and said, "Now teach me to shoot the bow."

Tree Wind took him to an opening and showed him how to pull the bow and place the arrow. Reed's arms were sore and it took him a while to get comfortable. He began to get the hang of it and started putting the arrows close to where he was aiming.

"You are a good teacher. I am ready," Reed said.

They walked back to the others and Reed sat close to Tall Tree.

"What do you plan to do?" Tall Tree asked.

"When it is dark, I will slip out and make a visit to the Apache camp. I plan to play with their minds a bit. If it works, you may not have to worry about them," Reed answered.

"The Apaches have superstitions," Shining Moon said. "They are more so at night."

They brought Haddok roasted venison and he stuffed it down. He then rolled up and slept for a couple of hours.

It was getting dark when he stripped off his clothes, wearing nothing but his drawers. He strapped on his pistol belt and walked to the small trickle running through their village. He cupped some mud and rubbed it on all his body except his legs. He would get them after he came out of the water when he left the valley. They walked him to the entrance. He went through it, bow and arrows in his hands.

33

Haddok came out from under the waterfall and stood in the waist deep water, scanning the area downstream. There was little moonlight. He saw nothing to alarm him. Moving across the stream, he slipped out on the west side. He stopped to apply mud to his legs.

He headed out north well away from the rock wall. He took his time and used his old method of walking a little and then stopping to listen. It was not long until he was far enough away from the waterfall to hear the night sounds.

The wind was blowing from the northwest and the leaves were rustling. The night was dark. As Reed walked quietly along, he chuckled a bit to himself, thinking about what he was going to try and do to the Apaches. It reminded him of some of the pranks he pulled on his sister as a little boy. He hoped this one worked.

Reed was beginning to feel better. Food and rest had replenished his strength. Walking was working the soreness out. He stopped suddenly when he heard a rustle in the leaves in front of him. He froze. He heard it again. He relaxed. It was only some small animal. Probably searching for food. Reed didn't know what it was, but he knew it was not a man.

He eased on out and continued his way north. Every now and then he could make out the sheer rock wall through the trees. He decided to stop and rest after a couple of hours on the trail. He didn't know what was in store and he wanted to be rested. He also wanted the Apaches to have plenty of time with the darkness before he got to them. Darkness can do strange things, especially if you are a little frightened.

The walking was easy and Reed was making good time. He had no way of judging how far he had come. He was thinking of stopping again to listen when he looked to his right and found the rock wall turning away from him. He figured he was getting close to the northern end. He walked toward the wall and pulled up quickly when he saw the glow of a campfire off to the left in front of him.

He knelt on one knee and thought about what he was going to do. He had a plan, but he had to be sure where they all were. He stood and walked toward the rock wall until he was up against it. The ground up there was littered with rocks and boulders. He could now hear the water roar as it fell into the hole.

Haddok climbed up on a big boulder and got a better view. They had three fires burning high. He could not see the Apaches. He dropped down and continued to walk around the base of the wall. He could see fire light shining off the rocks. He studied those rocks carefully, looking for a guard. He saw nothing.

He moved on until he came to the edge of the light. He climbed another boulder and could see the Apaches around their fires. They were up close to the fires and were facing toward the hole. They were about a hundred paces from the hole on the east side of the stream.

Reed dropped down to scout out a place to run to if he

needed it. He found a place some twenty-five paces back. It was a low group of rocks. They would serve as a good place to hunker down if the bullets started flying his way. He went to them and marked the fastest way there.

He then went back to the boulder he used earlier and climbed it. He rigged the bow and pulled it a couple of times. Without hesitation, he let an arrow fly in the direction of the campfires. He saw it fall and stick into the ground close to one of the fires. The Apaches saw it too.

About the time it hit the ground, he let another fly. It hit a few feet to the right of the first. The Apaches were getting to their feet and moving back into the darkness. Reed bellowed in a deep ghostly voice, "High kill wax the den." He dragged the sounds out as he did when learning the words.

It was quiet for a moment.

The Apaches started running through the fires on the way to their horses. They screamed and stumbled over each other. Not a single shot was fired. The sound of the stream falling into the hole muffled a lot of their sound, but Reed could see their actions. They were frightened and leaving.

Reed sat on the top of the boulder and laughed aloud. The mystery of Tall Tree did it again. He stayed there for a little while, listening to the roar of the water. He dropped to the ground thinking, I'm ready to go home.

34

Spotted Horse and his warriors rode into their village a little after daybreak. They were quiet. To a man they were happy to see the sun come up. The events around the hole and the shadows of darkness fueled their fright as they rode through the night. They fully expected He Who Runs With Spirits to come upon them while they rode. The warriors in the back of the pack had jostled all night. Nobody wanted to bring up the rear.

The people of the village became quiet when they observed the somber mood of the warriors. They expected a big victory celebration. They waited to hear the explanation. The warriors gathered around the fires to eat. The villagers gathered around Spotted Horse and listened.

He told the story. "He Who Runs With Spirits is not a real man. He is a spirit. He came out of the leather around his wrists without untying it. He killed seven of our men with a knife, even though he was wounded so bad he could not walk. He led us on a long journey. When we came up to him, a stream of water swallowed him before our eyes. We camped there to make sure he was gone. He came up out of the hole where the water swallowed him to shoot arrows into our camp. He screamed his name to us so we would know. No real man could have done this. I declare this day that He Who Runs With Spirits is no longer our enemy. Perhaps some day he will come to our campfires and talk. We could use such a friend in battle."

35

Haddok found most of the village waiting for him when he
returned to the valley. They were festive and walked with him to
the fire where Tall Tree was seated. Tall Tree explained their joy.

"Some of the men went to the mountain to look down upon
the place where the water hides. They saw what you did. They
told us how the Apaches ran in fear. You are a wise man Haddok,"
Tall Tree said.

"I'm glad it worked."

"It is the sign of a strong man when he chooses to spare
life. I know you can kill. The Spirit is with you."

"I don't know about that. I never have killed a man unless
I had to. I find no pleasure in it."

"By sparing their lives, you left them to tell the story. I
think they may stop looking for me."

"That's my hope. I've got a feeling your reputation is going
to spread through their people."

"Let us eat and enjoy the victory. Our women have been
cooking and we all have been waiting your return."

They brought bowls of stew and roasted venison. Reed dug

into his and they all ate together. Haddok looked around at the sight and thought, I'm mighty proud to have these people as my friends.

"What will you do now?" Tall Tree asked.

"I will leave at first light and go home. I have much work to do."

"How will you travel? You have no horse."

"I sent my horses home when I started trailing you. My friend Josh will come for me."

"Who is your friend?"

"He's a lot like you. I can always count on him. Maybe you can meet him some day."

Reed left out of the valley at daybreak. It felt good to be going home.

36

It was mid-morning as Reed climbed the mountain where he expected Josh to meet him. If the horses made it home, he figured Josh would give him a couple of days and then ride out to meet him. The place where they met earlier would be in Josh's mind. They both usually thought alike.

Reed did plenty of thinking as he walked. He was working on a plan to find Beecham. He also spent time thinking about Samantha. He had been so busy the past few days he hardly had time to think.

He moved to the top of the mountain and veered off the right toward the thick brush and trees where he and Josh had talked earlier. He slowed down as he came closer. Reed saw the horses first. Both were unsaddled and had their eyes dead on him. He moved a little closer and peered through the brush to see Josh on his back with his head on his saddle, hat covering his face. Reed slipped in and sat down across from him. He cleared his throat and Josh jumped like he'd been shot.

"How long you been here?" Josh asked.

"Oh, a couple of hours," Reed answered.

"You ain't done no such a thing. I ain't been asleep that long."

They both got up and gave each other a back slap and laughed.

"Man, you look like you've been in a scrap. What happened?" Josh said.

"Set down and I'll tell you."

Reed gave him the whole story.

"I wish I could have been with you to help," Josh said.

"Me too. There was a bunch of times I could have used you. How are things at the ranch?"

"Everything has been quiet. We haven't had any more people around after your hide. I hope you are ready to come home for a spell. There's two things I need to tell you that ought to make you hang around a while. First, me and Raven are getting married as soon as I can get you home. The preacher is just waiting on the word."

"I'm proud for you Josh. As soon as we get back, you can send him word and we'll get it on. I think Raven will make you a good wife."

"The other news is a letter we got from your father. It came on the stage addressed to you and we opened it. He and your sister are on their way to Prescott. He's sold his ranch in Texas and they are moving out here. He said for you to be looking out for a place he could buy here."

Reed couldn't control the joy that news brought. Paw and Tess here in Arizona with me, he thought. He couldn't wait to see them.

They talked on until they ran out of things to say and then saddled up and rode toward home.

37

Reed and Samantha sat their horses on their favorite high spot overlooking the Rocking H. The wedding was special. Raven was a beautiful bride. Josh was handsome in his new store bought clothes. The ranch below was still crawling with people. Many of the town folk came out for the wedding, along with friends from the other ranches. Most of the Diamond men were there. The ranch yard resembled a wagon train night stop. Reed and Samantha rode out after the wedding to steal a little time alone.

"Reed, I am so glad you were able to help your friend. I wish it was all over for you. I know you feel like you must find Loyd Beecham," Sam said.

"I've got to Sam. If I don't, then we will always be living on the edge. I hate to leave again."

"I was hoping we could get married before you leave. With your father and Tess on their way, why don't you wait? We could be married after they arrive and then you could go do what you must."

"I would hate to marry you and leave. What if I get killed?

"I don't care. I mean I do care. I don't want you to be killed.

It's just that I want to be your wife. I can handle anything that comes. I don't want to wait."

"I'll tell you one thing. I listened to that long winded preacher while Josh and Raven were being married and made up my mind I was going to shoot him before our wedding."

They both laughed and stepped down to stand close and enjoy the moment. Life was good for Reed Haddok.